STEREOTYPED*

VICK BREEDY

DEDICATION

I dedicate this book to Black Men who are stereotyped on a daily basis and to those that have faced adversity and bounced back.

Thank you, God for blessing me.
Thank you, family for supporting me.
Thank you, friends for encouraging me.
Thank you, readers for showing my books love.

VICK BREEDY

CONTENTS

STEREOTYPED*

VICK BREEDY

1
THE BLACK MAN

Elijah:

What woman with an ounce of common sense would willingly date a homeless man?

Women want a provider. They want a man that can keep them safe. Women want stability. They want to dine at fine restaurants, receive nice gifts and to be able to brag about their man to others. Women want a well-groomed confident man; a man that takes care of himself. They want their man to make them feel special. Women want to feel and be loved. They want loyalty and respect. Any woman, worth a damn, wants to be made love to inside of a bedroom, with the option to take the love making into other rooms. Women want real men. Period.

A homeless man can't provide shit! I know that this isn't breaking news. This isn't a secret. Homeless men are useless when it comes to providing. Admit it. The homeless are looked at and treated as the undesirables of this world. They are like the dog shit that you accidentally step into at the park when their irresponsible owner neglects to pick it up. Who wants to deal with someone else's shit? Nobody. That is why we are left in the parks, subways, street corners and back alleys to fend for ourselves. America doesn't want us. It doesn't matter that a large amount of us fought for the America that turned her back on us. We've lost limbs, risked our lives, lost our lives and our minds for the very people that loathe us.

Do you think of a courageous soldier when you think of us? No. When you think of the homeless, you think of that person with a specific potent funk. You imagine a disheveled and dangerous look. The sight of them makes you cringe. You roll your window up and lock your doors when you see them pandering during red lights or heavy traffic. You'll find plenty of the people that I'm referring to on the corner of Melnea Cass and Mass Ave. They are usually holding a brown cardboard sign designed to guilt you that reads something like *"God Bless You, Spare Some Change"* or *"It Is Better to Give Than to Receive"*.

Most, with a home to go to, cast judgement on the homeless and decide not to part with their spare change or singles. Most decide that they can't morally support the alcohol addiction or drug addiction that they diagnosed the undesirable with from within the confines of their driver's seat office. Then when the light turns green, they speed off with a Starbucks Grande Macchiato in their cup holder. They clearly have better things to waste their money on.

It is usually the woman that has little to give that gives the most. It is the women that have seen hard times themselves or have a family member that is suffering on some level. This is the woman that rolls down her window to offer kind words. When these women don't have money to give, because they are struggling themselves, they give unopened food that they had plans for or bottled water. Even with all that compassion, these women don't want a homeless man lying on top of them. They don't need any more takers in their lives.

That's what we do. We take. Therefore, I make it a point not to confuse the genuine kindness of Silvie with attraction.

Bless this day. Protect me from harm. Lead and guide my steps. Let me be grateful and not complain. Amen.

***

Today was unusually hot. It's mid-September. The weather in Boston tends to have bi-polar tendencies. You could be wearing a t-shirt in the morning and need a winter puffy coat by night. Tonight, it will probably be 30-40 degrees cooler. Whatever temperature it will be, I will be sleeping at the train station.

I usually roam the streets until late night. Then I find a dark corner inside of a train station entrance to rest my head for the night, with mice and rats as annoying roommates. The street rodents don't mess with me too much. They usually go around me when I'm lying in a corner that interrupts their route. Don't get me wrong, rats and mice are some nasty creatures, but I'm not afraid of them. Why should I be? They can't whoop me.

I never sleep at the same station two nights in a row. I may sleep at the Red Line Kendall Square stop one night and be at the Orange Line Forest Hills stop the next. I do this because I have to watch my back. One would think as a man who's homeless, I wouldn't have to worry about hating ass motherfuckers. Wrong. It doesn't matter that I don't have anything that anyone should be jealous of, there's always somebody that has less. They want whatever extra that you have that they don't. In my case, it's my integrity.

Some hate me because I still love myself, despite my circumstances. I know my worth and my current situation is not a reflection of my worth. That's how I carry myself. They are mad because I'm not out here doing petty crimes with them to make a buck. I'd rather try to wash up at a McDonalds and go stand with the Latinos outside of a nearby Home Depot at the crack of dawn and do an odd job for the day. I have one particular homeless colleague that isn't feeling me because of that. He thinks that I believe that I am better than him. His name is Slick. He'd be correct in his assessment of me. I'd rather be in these streets homeless than locked up. My current situation is just temporary. I know that God has more in store for me.

Are there women that I could probably stay with for a while until I get back on my feet? Yes. Will I do that? No. That is what got me into this situation. I was living with a woman that I thought I would one day marry. We were living together in her apartment. At first, I wasn't sure about living together. I was living with my roommate in Cambridge and our lease was almost up. My girlfriend was insistent that I moved in with her. I was hesitant but she said that it would help her out financially. I was in love so I moved in. I soon found out, I should have listened to my gut instincts. We lasted for a strong six months. I lost my job on month six. She put me out on month seven. By that time, my old roommate had moved out of the apartment we shared and moved on. My girlfriend and I both said some disrespectful things to one another; some no turning back things. I guess thirty days was too long to be out of a job. She put me out as soon as she found out that I didn't have my share of the rent money.

What was she expecting? She knew that I was out of work. Where did she think the money would come from? I am not the type of dude to start selling drugs or do some illegal shit to make ends meet. I had hoped, as my woman, she would hold me down. She had the nerve to tell me that she knew that I had money in a savings account and demanded that I give her money from it. I told her that I wasn't giving her my last. I wondered where her conscience went. How is she going to ask me for my last? She had a job to collect a check from. I didn't. That was the end of our story.

That was it. She put me out and I had no-where to go. I had no job to rely on for future income. All I had was a little over a thousand dollars in an Eastern Bank savings account. I took whatever could fit in a backpack and left everything behind. I had no-where to put my personal belongings that were large. I wasn't going to waste money paying for storage. My savings was going to have to last me until indefinitely.

That was three months ago.

Tonight, I am sleeping at Oak Grove Station. I took the last train. When I got off, I didn't follow the crowd to the exit. I went to my bedroom for the night—the sheltered bench on the platform. I've learned that if you don't present yourself as a drunk or an agitator the MBTA workers won't bother you. Only the low self-esteem assholes that have nothing better to do, give me a problem. You know the ones that talk all types of shit to make themselves feel more important. It takes all my self-control to keep myself from busting them in their head. Another place, another time….

Jean:

If you are having sex with a chick and she doesn't allow you to go down on her, peep game. She was fucking some other dude within the last twenty-four hours. I guarantee that! It's messed up, but that's not as scandalous as the chick I was dealing with as of last week. I thought that we were only seeing each other. I found out that I was the only one in the committed relationship when I went down on her and tasted latex.

Female number one at least has the decency to stop you from licking the remnants of her last partner. Female number two just doesn't give a fuck. She'll let you eat it and have no shame as she's pushing your head down. That level of bullshit I'm not trying to deal with. That's some selfish shit. She can't be doing some other dude and expect me to only be with her. If she just kept it real, we could've worked out an arrangement. Fuck that shit. As soon as I tasted the latex, I removed my head from the pussy and left the premises. That's some straight hoe shit.

As pro-black as I am, I'm really considering taking a break from black girls for a while. They sit and watch the same unrealistic reality shows and think it's ok to behave that way. That shit isn't the norm. We don't live in a world where you can freely act on your emotions and exhibit no self-control. You can't slap a bitch or pour a drink on one just because you're upset. That type of bullshit will get you fucked up real quick. White people already think of our women as ghetto, sassy, angry welfare moms. Why give them more ammunition?

I mention this because it's happened to me. I've dealt with this type of chick more than once. Here's how it happens. I meet a female. Her body is right. She smells nice. Her weave looks good. She acts sweet. She can hold a good conversation but doesn't talk too much. Everything feels right. Then I decide to bless her with the dick. Shit always changes after that. Now she has papers on me.

It happens slowly. She becomes a little more demanding then suddenly, has a motherfucking opinion about everything. She starts saying slick shit under her breath. Then she graduates to feeling free to talk shit out in public. I'll admit, if what's between her legs is that good, I'll put up with it for a while. It never lasts though. I get tired of hearing her mouth. She starts giving me the pussy less. I move on to the next one. There's always a next one. In my case, the next one is always a spin off from the last one. This shit gets old.

I need a partner. Someone that is going to bring something to the table besides a whole lot of mouth, good pussy and lies. I've already had that. I get mad every time I think about the one that had your boy in a short-term depression. She ruined it for all light skin women that may be looking for anything serious from me.

I need a dark skin woman that has a hustler's spirit. She must be about her paper. I don't want the kind of woman that wants my money. She has to want her own paper. I want to be able to brainstorm with her about ideas to build wealth. I want to feel like I can't make my next big move until I speak to my woman. I don't want a lying ass woman. I've already had her. I want something different. Where is she? Tell her to hit me up! As if on cue, my phone rings. Maybe it's her.

"What you doing?"

"Who's this?"

"Stop playing with your ignorant self. I need to borrow some money. I'll get it back to you when I get my money from Oliver's dad."

"Who are you kidding? You and I both know you don't get consistent child support from that sperm donor."

"Whatever Jean!"

"How much you need? It can't be that much if you're waiting on his payment to reimburse me. You and I both know how much he doesn't give you," I say laughing.

"I just need a hundred bucks. I need to pay for your nephew's school uniforms. Today is the last day to order. I thought I'd have his child support money by now."

"You call it child support, but unless it is enforced by the Department of Revenue, all you are getting is a stipend." She tries to speak but I cut her off. "Of course, I got you. And you don't have to reimburse me. That's my nephew. You are just going to have to explain to my newest boo that we can't go to Legal's Seafood. We may have to grab a meal at Popeye's instead." I say to my sister jokingly.

"Thank you, Jean. I really appreciate you coming through like this for me on such a short notice. I gave him the benefit of the doubt when I should have known better. I don't know what I'd do without you."

"I do. You'd be out there doing something strange for some change. That's what you'd be doing." I laugh. She giggles.

"I'll be by in an hour. I love you big brother."

"I love you too."

When she first started seeing him, I told her that he wasn't going to do right by her. I hang around enough no-good-motherfuckers to be able to identify one. He doesn't even have to speak. It isn't hard to smell a piece of shit. How my sister could keep stepping in it and not smell it remains a mystery to me.

My sister has been doing a good job raising my nephew on her own, but I know she struggles. I know that it is hard for her financially. She has a decent job, but let's face it; it is easier to raise a child on two incomes instead of one. She has such a big heart—too big if you ask me. She always sees the potential in people that don't see the potential in themselves.

Even with all she has going on she still makes time for others that she feels has it worse than her. My nephew and I have an 'Uncle-Nephew' day every other Saturday. Silvie thinks that I'm doing her a favor babysitting while she volunteers at a homeless shelter serving food. Honestly, I love spending time with my nephew. He needs a consistent male figure in his life. So, this kills three birds with one stone. Silvie gets to do her volunteer work, I get to spend time with my nephew and he gets that consistent male figure in his life. My sister only volunteers for four hours. I keep him the entire day , that way she could have some "me time." Sometimes, people just don't know how to stop—my sister included. They don't know how to press pause or take a break. I know the importance of self-care. I know first-hand, that if you don't take a break, something will break you. True story.

Shawn:

Today is the day that I am marrying the woman that I can't see my life without. I've finally experienced that feeling that so many people in loving marriages boast about. When you ask them how they knew that their spouse was "The one", their response is always the same; "You just know." Now I understand what that means. It's when the connection is undoubtedly strong and the relationship is easy.

In my case, my wife-to-be is who enters my mind as soon as I wake up and who I think about before I go to sleep. I think about her throughout the day and smile at something silly she said or did the day before. I don't make plans without considering her; not because she asks this of me—I do this because I want to include her in everything that I do or plan on doing. I've been waiting on her my entire dating life. I'm psyched that she chose me. I feel like I hit the Mega Millions! I'd choose her over hitting the lottery with no hesitation.

She truly is my better half. Her energy rejuvenates me. I always look forward to being in her company. She's a beautiful woman with a beautiful spirit. She's infectious. She's definitely got me under her spell. My boys are always cracking jokes. They swear that if my fiancée was out to pimp me, she could. I laugh with them because if her argument was compelling enough, she probably could.

I stand in the mirror looking at myself. Today, my "one" will take on my last name. I will gladly and publicly profess my love to the woman that I want to make babies with. I will tell the world that I will be everything she deserves and more. She has my heart. She is my heart. I'm looking forward to the next phase of my life. I'm so happy I could cry. On the low, I already did.

Peter:

How in the hell am I supposed to pay probation fees, child support and live? I swear I'm cursed. A brother just can't catch a break! What the hell do I go to work for? I don't come home with enough money to do anything. How the fuck am I supposed to do anything for me when I have to give all my money to D.O.R and the motherfuckers in the probation department. Folks wonder why I'm always in a bad mood. You'd be in a bad mood too if you had my life.

Today, I came home to another letter from the child support mafia threatening to suspend my license. Now, how in the hell am I supposed to pay child support if they take my license away. If I can't drive, I can't get to work. That makes no motherfucking sense to me. It's like I'm being punished because my previous relationships didn't work out. It's always the fathers that get the short end of the stick. The mother's act like fucking dictators and get to tell you when you can and can't see your kid. They dictate how often and how much men have to pay. We literally have to pay for making the bad decision of going raw in the wrong bitch. That's some bullshit! The worst part is the courts enforce the baby mama's bullshit.

Who the fuck monitors what they do with the money we give for child support? Is the D.O.R. doing checks and balances on where the money is going once they get our hard-earned money? They should have to send receipts for whatever it is that they use the money for. If the money is used for something like getting their hair done or nails done, the women should have to reimburse the dads. If they get a boyfriend or get remarried, we should automatically be taken off child support. I am sure it is women making the laws that govern this shit.

Women have it easy. All that they have to do is trap a man by getting pregnant and they have it made. They are set for the next eighteen years. Just thinking about it irritates the hell out of me. Both the mothers of my children get on my nerves. They act like bill collectors. They only call me for money. And that attitude of theirs....

What incentive is there to do better and strive for more? The more money I make, the more money they are going to take. If I don't make more, they can't take more. I got other shit that I need to take care of, not just child support—yet, these motherfuckers act like child support trumps all. The folks that do the math are dumb as hell. They do their calculations without keeping in mind that a man has to live. How am I supposed to take care of myself if I have to take care of these kids and their moms?

I've honestly had enough. My kids aren't suffering. They're not hungry—shit they probably eat better than me. Their moms are resourceful. It's time I get resourceful as well.

I'm going to quit. I'm going to quit this job after next pay period. I already got a new job lined up. That ought to allow me a few weeks for the child support mafia to lose my scent. It usually takes two to three checks for them to catch up with me. Two or three child support deduction free checks is the cushion I need right now. I figured it all out. Thank God only one of the mothers of my kids has the child support taken directly out of my paycheck. The other one allows me to bring it by every two weeks.

Jean:

My sister called me to say that her sperm donor pulled up to her house just as she was leaving to come to get the uniform money from me. She no longer needs to borrow the money and thanked me for being there for her. She told me that I could now take my boo out for seafood instead of fast food. I laughed at how crazy that sounded. A hundred dollars isn't going to make or break me. Sadness creeps up on me when I consider that a hundred dollars was so much more significant in Silvie's life.

This dude that my sister has a son with used to piss me the hell off. No…correction, he *still* pisses me the hell off. He's a weak ass dude. He's one of those people that can't admit when they are wrong. Instead, they flip it. They run game. They play the victim. Then they make the real victim feel like they did something wrong. Dudes like him never find fault in their own actions. They make it everyone else's fault. They truly believe their own bullshit.

This dude has no idea how good he has it. Do you know the type of headaches he doesn't have to deal with because he has a kid with my sister? My sister is not the 'You can't see your kid if you ain't paying child support' type of woman. Her main concern is him maintaining a consistent relationship with their son. She worries about her son's emotional well-being. He doesn't give a fuck.

He has gone six months without seeing his son and offered no justification. Meanwhile, his son plays make believe on an old cell phone pretending to talk to his dad. I witnessed it first-hand. "Don't you like me daddy?" he asked into my sister's Blackberry. His voice was soft and sounded insecure. That shit broke my heart. It made me want to go out and find the piece of shit, then do bodily harm. I stay out of it though. I offered to beat his ass, but she pleaded with me not to. I don't know what she ever saw in that dude. Her heart is too big. Most women would want their big brother to put a hurting on anyone that crossed them, especially when it comes to a child. Not my sister, her mentality is to let God handle it. That's not how you handle predators. In my book, you fuck them up before they fuck you over.

Shawn:

I'm excited about the wedding, but I'm more excited about the honeymoon. Nakia and I have been together for a year and a half. On our first date, I'll admit, I tried to hit it. She wouldn't let me. It wasn't for the reason that you think. She didn't tell me no because it was the first date, she told me no because she's a virgin. That disclosure was bittersweet. The pros are that she's a virgin. The cons are that she's a virgin.

Nakia is one of the rare women in her twenties that is saving herself for marriage. At the time, I had to decide if I wanted to be in this type of relationship. It was going to take a lot of self-control. I told myself that I'd give it shot. I wanted to see where things would lead. I'm glad that I did. Me giving us a shot has led us to the altar and later on, it will lead us to the bedroom.

You have no idea how *hard* it is to be in a relationship with a celibate woman. No pun intended. The hard part is that you have to be celibate too! Thoughts would race through my mind. What if the sex is whack? What if she doesn't give good head? I can't find out if its good or not until *after* I commit my life to her. What if I'm too big? Nah, that's more of a hope than a worry. The thoughts would drive me crazy until I realized one truth: I am getting a blank slate. She's not going to know if I'm good or not. She has nobody to compare me to. Knowing that information took away some of the anxiety that I was feeling about pleasing her.

Tonight, isn't only going to be a first for her. It will be my first time making love to a virgin. My boy told me that there's a psychological and emotional attachment that virgins have with their first. He said it's not always a good attachment. But, at the same time this is the same fool that told me to take it while she's asleep.

"Once I'm in there's no turning back. There's no good reason to wait until marriage," he said in a matter of fact manner.

I told him what he's referring to will get a brother jail time. I still remember the dumbfounded look on his face as we left the Apple store.

"What do you mean jail time?"

"Are you serious?" I asked, dumbfounded by his ignorance.

"Hell yah I'm serious. Why the mention of jail time?"

"Yea, JAIL TIME. Dude, what you just said is called RAPE!"

"It can't be rape if she's your girlfriend."

"Come on man you're playing right?"

I waited for about five awkward seconds for him to laugh. Nothing. This fool was as serious as a heart attack. There's no telling how many women he violated. I couldn't delve into that. I changed the subject before we ended our friendship over his bullshit. I sometimes question how he and I have been friends for all these years.

Today, I will marry the woman of my dreams. She's my soulmate. I'm in deep thought reflecting over our relationship She's my other-better-half. She's my heart. If someone asked me two years ago did I see myself being married two years down the line, I would have said "hell no" instead, I'm wearing my white tuxedo waiting in the room where they hold Sunday school. This isn't my church. This is her church home. She asked that we have our wedding ceremony at Zion Baptist Church in Lynn and I agreed. I would have found a way to marry this woman on Venus if that was what she wanted.

She and I decided that we'd separate ourselves from the wedding party an hour before the ceremony. She felt that we needed to have time with ourselves in solitude to reflect and mentally prepare ourselves for the next chapter in our lives. I would have preferred that my boys were in here with me, but I can see them later. I can't stop smiling. I'm mad happy yo! I can't wait to hit it. I didn't even do my daily self-love ritual this morning. That's my way of saving myself for her.

I wonder what she's doing. I told her that I would stay in this room for the entire hour, but I want to see her. I feel claustrophobic in this tiny room. This room is situated right next to the pool. I was told that this is the room that folks wait in before being called to take their baptismal dip. I know we're not supposed to see each other, but I can at least go talk to her, right? I know that she'll be upset but I can't resist. I decide to walk over to her room and just listen. Maybe I'll catch her singing to herself or hear her feet pacing. She'll probably still be getting ready. I'm not going to bother her. I just want to hear her.

Once I open the door, I see people entering the sanctuary. I say my hello's and give hugs as I try to make it to the other side of the church. She's in the basement where I've been told that they hold the other Sunday school class. I tiptoe down the steps that lead to where she's waiting for me. As badly as I want to see her and tell her I love her I don't. Instead, I sit down on the steps and just listen.

At first, it's quiet. I can hear her high heels walking around, but that's it. It's comforting to hear her familiar footsteps. That means that she hasn't changed her mind. She's in there and ready to live the rest of her life with me. I'm going to do everything within my power to make sure that she has everything that she wants. I want my wife to experience nothing but happiness with me.

I get up to head back to my room. Just as I stand up, I hear her phone ring. I decide to wait just so that I can hear her voice.

"Stop calling me," she says firmly. That gets my attention. I stick around to see who is irritating my soon-to-be wife.

"So what! You know damn well you were a mistake. This is my wedding day. Don't be calling me with this shit. You should be ashamed of yourself. How do you manage to get your best friend's fiancé pregnant? I'm terminating this pregnancy as soon as I come back from my honeymoon. You don't run this. I do! This is my body." I hear her scream into the phone. "I better not what? Oh, you threatening me now? Here's something I can guarantee. If you tell Shawn, best believe I will fuck your life up. Oh... you're that grimy that you'll hurt your best-friend because you're mad at me." *Did she just say best friend?* "How the fuck am I supposed to explain a pregnancy when I'm a virgin?"

I was on the other side of the Sunday school door shocked. You know that expression people use when they say that they couldn't believe their own ears? It's only now that I understand what that means. We often use it in a generic way to express that the information we heard was surprising. To truly not believe your own ears is a lot more than it just being surprising. You are in a state of shock that takes you outside of yourself while you watch yourself listen to the information. Then it becomes an argument between yourself and your outside self.

That feeling you get when you're so shocked that you see yourself outside of yourself—that's where I'm at. I see myself breaking down the door and choking the fuck out of her. She won't have to abort her baby because she won't be alive to make that decision. An image of my fiancé taking dick from my best friend floods my mind. Before I know it, I'm beating this raping ass motherfucker down. These thoughts happen within about ten seconds. Before I lose control, I snap out of it.

For the moment, I am myself. The weight of what I just overheard crushes me. My heart races and drops to my gut. A lump forms in my throat. I feel nauseous. I hear myself making an uncomfortable involuntary wail as all the contents of my stomach eject out of my mouth. I vomit right there on the stair case.

Nakia opens the door. She must have heard me because when I look up I see her standing in front of me looking absolutely stunned. She's confused. I know she's wondering what's up. She's wondering if I heard her disgusting disclosure. She better not dare ask. For the first time in our relationship, I don't look at her. I look through this seemingly beautiful creature one last time before I walk away from her and my vomit without saying a word.

I don't get very far, before I hear a familiar voice. He stops me. l

"I can't believe the shit that I just heard." I turn around and see him. *How long was he standing there?*

"What? You didn't hear anything," I say failing at my attempt to ignore him.

"I'm not deaf? You know I heard that shit!"

"I don't know what you're talking about. What did you hear?" I didn't know that he was standing behind me witnessing my life fall apart.

"Your wife-to-be spread the very legs she been locking shut with you to another dude. On top of that she's pregnant. You ain't even got close enough to sniff it and he hit it then knocked it up!"

How does he know Nakia hasn't been giving me any? I deny it.

"You don't know what you're talking about. She would never do that. You must have heard her wrong. My wife-to-be is a virgin."

"You better stop acting deaf and dumb and do something. Why don't you kick in the door or something? I can't believe you're just standing here looking crazy!"

"She wouldn't do that to me…he wouldn't do that to me," I say more to myself. My vocal bystander walks away shaking his head.

I leave without saying a word to anyone else. Peter catches me driving off. I see him but keep on going. He yells my name. I hear him, but because of the mental and emotional state that I am in, I can't stop or respond to him. What I need is to get the hell out of here and that's what I do. I drive off without looking back. A voice comes to me—my own voice. I am in a daze, but the voice is loud and clear. He calls me a weak ass excuse for man. He tells me that I played myself. I do my best to ignore it. I pray that one day I can look at this experience as a blessing. Right now, I can't see that far.

Peter:

Where did this dude disappear to? How are you going to be late to your own wedding and you're already in the building? We saw each other an hour ago. He was all set. He didn't have to add any finishing touches to his make up like Nakia did. All he had to do was sit his fat ass down and wait. This dude has everything going for him and he goes and does this—just vanish. What's worse is, nobody can find him; he's not answering his phone.

He's spoiled and doesn't even know it. That shit eats me up. He lives a good life. He has a good job. There are no child support checks he's responsible for. He owns his own house and now, he's getting married to a dime. He should have no complaints. I honestly don't know what she sees in his fat ass. We met her on the same night, but she foolishly chose him. I can't say that I wasn't in my feelings about that decision. I don't know what she saw in him over me.

Shawn is about five nine or five ten, average height. Last time I checked, he weighed two hundred and thirty pounds. He has a good fifty pounds on me and I'm six one. I'll give it to him, he did try to lose weight for his wedding. He looks like he has lost a few pounds. His gut isn't protruding as much as it usually does—but this dude is still big. He has always been a big dude with a square shape.

As a kid, he would wear clothes that were too tight for him. As an adult, he still does. He is the type of dude that needs a 2x button up shirt but puts on a 1x. If that's not bad enough, he has the nerve to tuck the shirt in like he has a waistline. As his boy, I tried to tell him that he's up in these streets looking crazy. He just thinks I'm hating on him. If he lost that fat and hit the weights, he'd give me a run for my money. He's not an ugly dude and despite his size he gets females. I guess there's a market for the teddy bear look.

I figure he's in his car with cold feet so I decide to go knock some sense into him. I'm walking through the church's heavy backdoor to the parking lot. The lot is packed. It is shared with a Latino supermarket so it's hard to tell which cars are here for the wedding and which cars are here for the grocery store. I don't know exactly where he parked, but I know his car anywhere. He drives a black Cadillac Crossover and I must admit his ride is clean.

Usually it would be easy to find, but this lot is beyond capacity. People made their own makeshift spots when they ran out of places to park.

As I stand outside of Zion's back door, I spot him. He's leaving. *Where the fuck is he going?* I contemplate jogging over to where he's parked. I decide to yell from the door instead. I am not running in this suit.

"Yo, Shawn!" I yell. He doesn't hear me, or maybe he does. I don't know and from where I am standing I can't tell. Doesn't look like this wedding is going to start on time, if at all. I can't imagine what the hell happened to have him driving away from the perfect girl. Nakia is the perfect girl. She's a light skinned black woman. Her hair is long, black and straight like an Asian woman, but when it's wet it curls up like Latina hair. She got a body like that actress Meagan Good—petite just like her. Her face is just as impressive as her body. She looks like a lighter version of Sanaa Lathan; if I didn't know her I would think they were sisters. Nakia is fine! And she's a virgin. Correction—was a virgin.

I can't say I haven't imagined what it would be like if I became her first. There's something holy about virgin pussy. It's like a spiritual awakening once you get inside. Makes you want to say "Amen" and give God thanks. You get to go where no man has gone before. I don't know any man that doesn't fantasize about having a virgin. They are lying if they say they haven't.

2

NOBODY'S SAMBO

One Month Later…

Elijah:

I wake up to what sounds like the police knocking on my door with an arrest warrant. I jump up only to realize that I was sleeping. When my eyes focus, I am looking at a face that is unfamiliar to me. I know the MBTA staff at this station. This person that is standing in front of me, with a look of disgust, is definitely new. He must be new to this station, but not new to the position. I say this because in the three seconds it took me to focus, I've assessed that he is an arrogant prick. What's worse is that he stinks!

His cologne is overbearing. He smells as if he substituted his lotion for cologne. He reeks. I know I have my days when my body odor is not on point but I do the best I can with what I have or don't have. It's hard out here in these streets. I don't know this dude's story, but I know he didn't sleep on the street last night. I never trust dudes that use a lot of cologne. I feel like they are the types that are hiding something. They're either trying to cover up their funk or trying to hide their insecurities and need for attention. This dude is probably using cologne because he doesn't have anything about him worth remembering. I already don't like this dude. With all that cologne, I know he's hiding something. His posture is irritating me. He's standing there like he's going to do something.

"This isn't a motherfucking motel," he says with a scowl on his face.

I say nothing as I keep eye contact with him, picking up my backpack that served as my pillow.

"Hurry the fuck up!" He continues to yell. "Don't nobody want to see your ass out here first thing in the morning. Folks are trying to get to work...where you should be. Instead you all laid up out here like this is your motherfucking apartment. Don't let me catch your bum ass out here again!"

It takes every ounce of self-control that I have not to push this dude onto the tracks. Who the hell does he think he's talking to? I stand up straight and grill him down, barely blinking. We are about the same in height and weight. He talks like he can back up his shit but he ain't no killer. I know his type—all noise. His bark is stronger than his bite. Those that bark really don't want to bite and those that bite don't give a warning—they just bite.

I can see that he is uncomfortable with my silence. He's fidgety. He doesn't know what to do with himself because he is expecting me to be combative. In my experience, no response is always a strong response.

The sound of the approaching train breaks our standoff. I walk off. Behind me, I can hear him talking shit. He's no longer swearing, but still shit talking. I continue walking. The doors open and a crowd of people get off the train. As I walk down the stairs, I feel my head pounding. I'm not sure if it is from the unwelcomed encounter or because of something else. In my bag, I reach for the travel size bottle of ibuprofen. When I first bought it, the bottle came with ten capsules of 200mg pills, now, I'm down to five. I decide to hold off and wait. It could just be dehydration. I will get some water soon but for now I have to get to a bathroom. I try my best not to make urinating in the streets an alternative to a public bathroom. I've only had to do that one time.

I knew that I shouldn't have held off on going to the bathroom when I had a chance to use it at the shelter but I was too busy helping with the volunteer staff. How I see things, since I get free meals there, I show my appreciation by paying it forward. Any time that I eat there, I help them break the tables down and do anything that requires heavy lifting. I like to think that I do what men should do. We should do the dirty work to spare the women.

Most of the volunteers at the shelter are women. I know that they appreciate my help. They don't have to tell me, although they do. The truth is, I enjoy being in their company. Although I am not a part of their conversations, I hear them. I feel like I'm at a private viewing of that sitcom *Girlfriends*. These women are funny as hell. Being in their company lifts my spirits.

One day I was helping them shut down and I heard one of them complain. She said that it's messed up that the bathroom is shut down and they had to wait until they got home to pee. I must have missed that memo because my plan was to go to the bathroom when I was done. The closest public bathroom wasn't close enough and that day I had consumed two bottles of water. One, I had with my meal and the other I finished half-way through my voluntary shift. By this point I was ready to explode. It seemed the need to urinate became even more urgent when I heard that I couldn't use the bathroom. It was like my bladder said "Oh well, we're just going to go right here."

I waved goodbye to them and quickly made my way out the door. I knew that I wasn't going to be able to hold it. I had no choice but to go in between two sedans in the parking lot. I felt like a nasty dude but it was either that or urinate on myself. I didn't want to make a fellow T-rider suffer or should I say suffocate if they happen to be next to me on the train. In between the cars was the lesser of two evils. To add another layer to my new low, I had to stand there for at least a minute straight. This wasn't a quick embarrassing act. It felt like I was letting out a gallon as I simultaneously looked around to see if anyone could see me.

When I was done, I looked inside my back pack. It had seen better days. I pulled out the bottle of water that was supposed to hold me over for the rest of the day. I then poured the entire bottle of Poland Springs over the area of cement where I released my bodily fluids. That's the best I could do to clean up. That was the first and hopefully the last time I'll ever have to use the bathroom outside. I'll never wait until the last minute again. Lesson learned.

I usually keep an empty water bottle with me. I try to drink three to four sixteen-ounce bottles of water a day. When my bottle becomes empty, I fill it up in whatever public restroom I use. You have to stay hydrated. Water is everything. The only real balanced meal I get is from the shelter. There's no doubt that I've lost weight living out here on these streets. I was bulkier before. I'm still in good shape, I'm just leaner. Living out here, I've developed a routine. Having a routine keeps me sane; routines give me a sense of comfort.

My routine was disrupted this morning with the overly zealous T-worker. Usually, the arrival of the first train is what awakes me. I make sure that I'm sitting up straight on the bench by the time people start getting off the train. I do this because I don't want people complaining about the homeless man sleeping on the bench. Once everyone leaves and heads downstairs to the exit, I do my three-minute calisthenics routine. It consists of push-ups, sit-ups and mountain climbers. After that, I sit with my notepad and figure out what I'm going to do to get myself closer to my goal. I have several small goals; but ultimately, my goal is to be off these streets with a good job and an affordable place to live. There are several steps I must take to set myself up to be in a position to obtain the bigger goals. To do that I use the one place I know I can get a clear focus—the library. I spend a large part of my day in the library.

The first stop that I make in the morning is to the closest McDonalds or Dunkin' Donuts. I buy a large hot coffee. I prefer the taste of Dunks, but the price of Mickey D's. Location usually dictates which one I go to. For instance, this morning I'm at Malden Station. Dunks is right across the street so that's where I'm headed. I walk into Dunks and head straight to the bathroom. This particular bathroom is marked as gender neutral. I find that gender neutral bathrooms tend to be cleaner than men only bathrooms. Women will complain to management about a dirty bathroom. Men don't have high expectations of public restrooms. I quickly brush my teeth and empty my bladder only. I'll handle my other business later.

In less than three minutes I'm out of the bathroom and get in line. I order my regular.

"Medium hot caramel swirl coffee with cream and no sugar please."

"Will that be all?" the cashier asks.

Her breathe smells like cigarettes and her teeth are yellow. She has wrinkles all over her face. She looks like she is at least sixty years old. I smile at her.

"Yes. That's it. Thank you." I have cash on me, but I hand her my debit card. She tells me that the card reader isn't working. I guess cash it is. I keep twenty dollars on me in cash at all times. It is only for emergencies. I don't pay for anything with cash. Any money that I make, I put it into my bank account. I don't feel comfortable using cash. If my debit card ever gets stolen, the bank will process it as fraud and I'll get my money back. That can't happen if I get cash stolen from me. I'd rather be safe than sorry.

After a few minutes, I get my coffee, find a table and sit down. First thing in the morning, I like to read fiction; it's my temporary escape. I always have a book in my backpack. Today's read is *Bitter* by Vick Breedy. I'm only on the third page and I can't put it down. I've heard that it's going to be turned into a movie. That, I would love to see. I'm not sure when it's supposed to come out. I have no money to splurge on a movie anyway. In my opinion, the books are usually better than the movies.

I sip on my coffee and set my alarm on my phone to read *Bitter* for an hour. I don't want to wear out my welcome. I stick to that rigid hour no matter how good the book is. This morning, I'll admit, it is hard to stop reading. It's as if I'm pulled into the book itself. As I get ready to flip the next page the alarm brings me back to reality. I can't believe an hour has passed already. I read the last sentence and place a piece of napkin in the spot where I left off as a bookmark. I shut the alarm off and wipe the table to rid it of any coffee I may have spilled. I make it a point to say goodbye to the Dunks staff as I leave and thank them. The young Latina making the coffee smiles at me and the cashier waves goodbye. Having a rapport goes a long way. My grandmother taught me that. People treat you with kindness when you go out of your way to engage with them, even if it is only a "hello" or a "thank you." It's that simple.

I make my way down Centre Street to get to the Malden Public Library on the corner of Main and Salem street. I make it a point to have a library card for each city that I frequent. My wallet is full of library cards, an ID and an Eastern Bank debit card. I'm hoping to add a health insurance card to the mix sooner than later. My health has been good and I want it stay that way. Healthcare is priceless.

It's still very early. This library doesn't open until 9am. It's only 6:30am, which means I have over two hours to wait. It's a little chilly outside, but I'm still warm from the coffee. That coffee served as my breakfast. I won't be hungry until lunch. Since I have a lot of time to kill, I walk back up to Malden square and find a place to sit and read. I know I can finish this book by the time the library opens so that's exactly what I will do.

***

The book was raw and off the chain! It's a must read. I hope this library has the *Bitter Trilogy*, I need to take out the sequel, *Still Bitter*. I'm dying to find out what Ava does next. I look down at my phone and it is a little after nine o'clock. I stuff the book back in my bag an make my way towards the library entrance. Besides the librarians and other staff, I'm the only one here. I go through the double doors and hurry to the bathroom. It is time to empty out what I was too uncomfortable to do in Dunks gender neutral bathroom. The men's bathroom is usually empty first thing in the morning. This is great for me because I'm able to dookie in peace. I will admit this is one of the luxuries I took for granted before I became homeless.

Peter:

It's Friday and I'm feeling good. I followed my gut and quit my job on Wednesday. Today, I got a call to start training for a new job on Monday. I had the option to start Monday or three weeks from Monday. I'm not missing that good T money. I told them that I'd be available to start that Monday. That was a month ago. It's also been a month since the wedding that I spent my hard-earned money on buying a bridal shower gift, renting a suit to be in the wedding and giving a card with a check for seventy-five dollars. All of that was for nothing because that fool didn't get married.

He bounced. He didn't answer or return anyone's calls for days. I thought that was pretty selfish of him to leave us all hanging like that. Nakia had her sister announce, in so many words, that the wedding was over before it started and that there would be no reception. I was pissed. I already passed in my *Congratulations You're Married* card with the rest of the bridal party. There was no getting that back. I was also pissed that Shawn didn't give me a heads-up. He didn't text or call me. I mean, damn, I thought we were boys.

When he finally got back to me, it was through text. I still haven't spoken to him. He did tell me what happened, but he doesn't know who she cheated on him with. Supposedly, Shawn overheard a conversation that he wasn't supposed to hear. Nakia not only cheated on him, but she got pregnant too. I told that fool that he didn't need to be celibate just because she said she was. That hoe straight lied to him. She didn't look like no virgin to me anyway. She had his gullible ass fooled, but not me. It's one thing to cheat, it's another thing to cheat and get pregnant; but, it's a whole other offense to say you're a virgin, make your man wait until marriage to get some and then have him find out you're having a baby with the dude you *didn't* make wait.

Bitches ain't shit.

I knew that she'd let me hit it. I didn't plan on being the dude that impregnated her though. Who knows if it's even mine.

Men cheat. Period. If women don't believe that by now, they're crazy. Men love women so much that they can't have just one. I cheated on both of my baby mamas and they both left me because of it. They were both pregnant a month apart from each other.

As soon as my daughter was born, his mother had me summoned to court to start paying child support. Her bitter ass tries to punish me whenever she gets the opportunity to. Do you know that she even has a black hoodie that she wears that says BITTER written across the chest with bold white lettering? She's crazy.

My son's mother is the exact opposite. Honestly, I had no reason to cheat on her—she just started to become boring. During her first trimester, all she did was complain. She was always nauseous, always tired and she never wanted to fuck. This got me to thinking that if she was like this in her first trimester, she was going to be even worse in the second and third. No man has any time for that. I started staying away longer and going out more often. She got suspicious and found out that I was sleeping with my daughter's mother, Patrice.

I didn't deny it when she called me on it and when she broke up with me, I didn't put up a fight. I was tired of her anyway. I secretly hoped she would have an abortion, but I knew she wouldn't, so, I didn't even bother bringing it up. I thought things would get easier since I was down to one woman. As my luck would have it, Patrice ended up finding out that I had a Jump Off. She didn't care that the woman was just a someone that I hit up from time to time when I needed a change of pace.

It is my fault that I lost Patrice; I was getting sloppy. Instead of going home, my dumb ass went to Patrice's apartment drunk. I was so drunk, I wasn't even aware that I was marked up. I had hickie's all over my neck and chest. This crazy baby mama of mine waited until I fell asleep, then she went into the freezer and took a tray of ice out. I didn't even stir when she lifted the waistband of my briefs; however, the scream that I let out when I felt the ice hit my balls was unrecognizable. Never have I been caught so off guard. She poured the entire tray of ice inside my briefs. That shit was cold as hell!

Looking back at it, that shit was kind of funny. My Jump Off knew what she was doing. She knew that I was tore up. She wanted more of "my time". What she failed to realize was that my time was already split up between Patrice and Silvie—I had none left for her. This was her way of getting back at me. Although it was fucked up, her tactic worked. She put me in a position where the women I was giving my time to would no longer want me. That way, she could get all my time. It worked in the beginning. Unfortunately for her, the more time I spent with her, the more I realized that she was my Jump Off for a reason. I could only deal with her for short periods of time. If we weren't having sex, I had no desire to be around her. We didn't last long. After that, I thought about trying to hit Silvie up, but changed my mind.

To this day, Silvie doesn't interact with me. If I don't drop off the child support, she doesn't call asking where I'm at. Let me rephrase that. Silvie doesn't stalk me like Patrice does for money. She asks and I get back to her when I have time. I let her know what I have and when I'll be able to swing by. That's how we operate.

I never really bonded with my son while he was a baby. Now he's six and I don't know where to begin. Don't get me wrong, I see him when I drop off money, but I don't spend any one-on-one time with him. Who knows what lies his mother has been feeding him about me. She's mad because I stood her up a few times. I told Silvie to tell my son that I would come spend time with him but it seems I just had bad luck. Each time that I planned on it, something else came up. It doesn't make me feel good to let down a kid, but shit happens. He'll get over it.

I've been working for the T for a month now. It's a good job with good benefits. My child support payments that get deducted from my check don't even hurt as much as it used to. I honestly can't complain too much about the job. I got sent to work at Malden station yesterday. I almost had to whoop this bum's ass. The piece of shit was sleeping on a bench on the platform like it was his crib. These homeless motherfuckers got some balls on them. They cop an attitude with you as if you are in the wrong. This one got up mad slowly when I confronted him. He was mean mugging me the entire time. He looked like he wanted to try me but he had enough sense not to and kept it moving.

That was my morning.

Shawn:

It's been a month since I found out about Nakia's pregnancy. I don't know if she's keeping it or not—it doesn't matter to me anyway. It's not like there is a chance that the child could be mine. It is not humanly possible. The only person I know that was able to impregnate a woman without hitting it, named his son Jesus. Since I'm not God, the likelihood of this child being mine is zero percent.

I didn't want to drag anything out. I knew that there would be questions, but I underestimated the amount. My Facebook page was flooded with inquiring minds and unsolicited comments. These Facebook "friends" are nosy as hell. That's what I can't stand about social media. If you post your highs, they are going to want to be informed of your lows. I didn't answer any of their questions, however I wanted to make a point. I knew it was petty, but I didn't care. I logged into my Facebook account and changed my status: "WHEN YOU FIND OUT THE HONEYMOON HAPPENED WITHOUT YOU…," and I left it at that.

That was a Friday night. Saturday morning when I logged back in to check my notifications, I realized how big that small comment was. It had over a hundred comments and almost two hundred likes. Damn these people are nosy. I skimmed through the comments. There were a few shocked emoji's, some left condolences like someone died and others wanted to know the details. I didn't answer any. Let them keep wondering. Instead, I went on Nakia's page to look at her posts.

I know it wasn't the smartest thing to do. I knew I was setting myself up to get hurt all over again, but I needed to see. I needed to know if it was just one dude or more. I wanted to check her comments, see if there was any man that consistently liked her posts. Maybe see if I missed any clues. Right now, I wish I had a friend like Carly Red from *Love and Hip Hop*. This is the type of digging she's known for doing. I imagine her checking to see if maybe he said some slick shit that I didn't pay attention to. Who knows how many men she let hit it. Virgin my ass! I was in detective mode.

Unfortunately, I wasn't able to get far. When I got to her page the icon to send her a friend request was unavailable. This means she unfriended me, and possibly even blocked me. That pissed me off.

I was angry but I wasn't about to let Nakia hurt my heart and my wallet. So, instead of sulking, I went to work that Monday—the day I was supposed to start my honeymoon. I didn't want to waste any vacation days depressed at home. Work was the distraction I needed. My boss was surprised to see me when I arrived at the office. Before going to my cubicle, I went into her office and told her what happened. I left out the part about Nakia playing me. I thought it was wise not to tell her that Nakia had me masturbating during the entire relationship because she claimed to be a virgin. I didn't tell her that not only wasn't she a virgin, but she got herself a bun in the oven. I also left out the part that Nakia had the nerve to show up in a white dress knowing her promiscuous ass should have been wearing brown. Brown would have matched the bullshit she put me through this entire time.

Nope. I didn't tell my boss any of that. Instead, I told her that we decided that we weren't ready and cancelled the wedding. It was best to leave out the part that it got cancelled *during* the wedding. After telling my half-truth, she believed there wasn't much drama involved. Although I left out a lot of details, I knew telling her was in my favor. She was sympathetic and shielded me from any nosey co-workers wondering why I was at work when I should have been on my honeymoon. I got a few stares, but no one mentioned anything. I'm sure it was because of an influential email drafted by my boss that I was blind copied on.

That was two weeks ago. Today I am sitting on my bed with my laptop on my lap. I'm dressed in white boxer briefs and a navy-blue robe because I am working from home. I have a conference call in the next five minutes. The presenter will be sharing his desktop with us, which means I'll also have to log into Skype for this meeting. We were given a conference call-in number and told not to accept the audio option on Skype because it gives off too much feedback. This meeting is about updates on the new portal that we launched. I'm glad I'm not in the office. I can take part in this meeting virtually.

There's at least thirty minutes left of a reality TV show that I've been binging on. I know that I am depressed—I wouldn't be watching this type of stuff if I wasn't. I watch for a few more minutes. When I look at the clock I notice that it's almost time for my call. Time has gone by quickly. I find the remote and press pause right when it looks like there's going to be some conflict between one tattoo artist and an unhappy customer.

I have a reputation for being good with systems and data. I'll have to do a little bit of a presentation during this meeting to explain the new updates that have been put in place to track adherence. The PowerPoint presentation is being shared remotely by the first presenter's desktop. After about ten minutes, my name appears on the slide. That's my prompt to get ready to talk about how the company is losing revenue and show them the tools I created to target the areas that have the most potential for low adherence.

I've been on mute this entire time. Unlike many of my colleagues, I remember to take myself off mute before talking. There are a few known to talk to a telephonic audience and forget to take themselves off mute. I never want to show them any areas of incompetence. I don't have the luxury of making a minor mistake that would get laughed off if I was white. As a black man, I have to be hypervigilant about making sure I'm perceived in a competent and positive light. I complete my portion of the presentation.

"Does anyone have any questions?" I ask but hope that they don't.

"Yes Shawn. First, I want to thank you for all the work you've done to create this data. It is going to make our jobs a lot easier and our work more efficient. Most importantly it will help us with increasing our revenue. My question is-"

"Fuck that shit! You're a fucking liar! You fucked her just admit it!" I hear the TV blare.

I shrink inside of myself. My leg accidently hit the remote control and what was once on pause is now blaring through my bedroom. *Shit.* I frantically try to shut the TV off before my entire department hears any more of the "ratchetness" I was watching before the call. What could I do? I am the only one on the phone working from the comfort of their bedroom; I can't pretend that it didn't come from my end. All I can do is apologize and laugh it off as being one of the hazards of working from home. I cringe because I know I have just tarnished their perception of me. I ask again if there are any other questions. Nobody responds in the three awkward seconds I give them to ask their question. I thank them and the next person starts their presentation. I zone out for the rest of the call.

When the conference call ends, we all say our goodbyes. I was on the line after my presentation however, I have no idea what was discussed after. I was completely checked out. Lately, I haven't been in the best of moods , but that remote-control mishap really set me off. I was caught off guard and embarrassed. Although it had nothing to do with my wedding day, it reminded me of how I was caught off guard when I overheard Nakia's phone conversation.

Jean:

I can't stand it when a white person goes out of their way to use slang because they think that is my "native language". I get it. They are trying to develop a rapport and want you to know that they have no problem with black people. They want you to know that they are one of the cool ones, the tolerant ones, the ones that aren't racist. They don't get that the very act of searching through their mental rolodex of words to use with 'niggers' is in fact racist behavior. The assumption that you have to make a linguistic shift because we couldn't possibly bond over a shared intellect and mastery of the English language is racist as fuck.

ATTENTION WHITE PEOPLE: STAY WHITE. It's ok. Unless your name is Jay and you grew up in the projects where you were the minority and your best friends' names are Craig, Taharri and Damal, don't come at me like that. Stay in your lane and your native tongue. This happened to me this morning; but because I enjoy my paycheck and the flexibility my job offers, I didn't go off. The previous Director resigned and was replaced by the current one—

the same person I chose not to go off on. I may be "woke" by I'm not stupid. I need my health insurance.

I've learned how to play the game in white corporate America. Every time I feel my inner W.E.B Dubois trying to break free, I pull out the copy of *The Souls of Black Folk* that I keep in my desk drawer. Every black man should have a copy of this book. When you think the white folks are driving you crazy, know that there's a reason why you feel this way. It's that double consciousness that we deal with. If you don't know what I'm talking about look it up. In the basic sense of the term, it means that black people have a hard time unifying their black self with their American self. We have a divided identity. Our shit is complicated.

Speaking of complicated, I met this sexy little thing while I was at the Starbucks not far from my job in Kendall Square. Her name is Suzie...Sexy Suzie. She was staying at the Marriott connected to the building Starbucks is in. Fortunately for me, she was forward as hell. I like that though. I like a woman that knows what she wants and goes for it. The day we met, Sexy Suzie came over to the island where the sugar is kept. That's where I was standing. She made eye contact with me and didn't break it. After a few short moments of silent flirting, she did what I never would have expected.

"You single?" Sexy Suzie asked breaking the silence. She was not shy.

"Yup."

"Do you think I'm sexy?" She asked as I openly stared at her cleavage.

"Yup," I said with a Cheshire Cat grin on my face.

"That's good because I'd be lying if I told you that I wouldn't be willing to sleep with you on the first date," she said as she inched closer to me. An older Hispanic woman stood beside the table ear hustling. We went on as if she was not there stirring sugar into her coffee.

"Is that so? Well, I'd be lying if I said I wouldn't be looking forward to our first date. You got a name?" I asked.

"Suzie," she answered seductively.

"Nice to meet you Sexy Suzie," I said and then handed her my card. There was no need to play games.

"Does this number receive text messages?" She asked.

"The bottom number is a cell phone. You can text that phone. Be discreet though, it's a company cell phone," I warned her.

"Oh honey, I'll be discreet. There is nothing that I want to talk to you about anyway. I'll be texting you a time and a place. No need for chit chat," she said with a smirk before walking away.

It was as if suddenly I had x-ray vision. In my mind, I could see what her ass looked like bare. I imagined that she had on a black lace thong under that tight pencil skirt she was rocking. As I watched her walk away only one thought came to mind. *She's definitely getting this dick.*

That was two days ago. Today is our third day in a row meeting for lunch. She is here for a weeklong conference. I've learned a lot in the three days we've been seeing each other or should I say doing each other? If you remember, she asked me if I was single, but I didn't ask her if she was. Once I found out what page she was on, whether she was single or not didn't matter. She signed up for the dick only. And that's what she gets from me…dick. We talk a little after we've taken care of business, not too much though. It's more of a matter of fact conversation. On day three, I head over to the Marriott during my lunch break where we meet up.

"I'm about to leave. You good or do you need another round?" I say half-jokingly.

"I'm more than good. When Baxter gets back I'll be all set," she says as if I'm familiar with that name.

"Baxter?" I repeat.

"Yes. He's usually ready to fuck after a long day at a meeting. Since I've already been satisfied by you, I won't be disappointed by the twenty pumps his sixty-seven-year-old dick provides."

"Twenty pumps? Sixty-seven-year-old dick? Are you saying that you're taking it from an elderly man?"

"It's so funny that you use the phrase 'taking it', because that's exactly what I'm doing. I'm taking his twenty pumps, so that I can take his money out the bank whenever I please."

My eyes widen in surprise. I never took her to be shy, but damn. Noticing the look on my face she let out a laugh and continued.

"I'll sacrifice old dick for good old fashion cash any day of the week. He provides me with the lifestyle that I want to live. I provide him with the confidence men love when they have a fine young thing like me on their arm. They like to be envied by other men. More importantly, they like how their old wrinkled, damn near flaccid, dick feels inside pussy that's forty years younger than them."

She then goes inside of her purse and puts a stack of twenty-dollar bills inside of my jacket pocket.

"Thanks for a great couple of days. Baxter and I will be flying back to D.C tonight. I'll be sure to hit you up whenever I come back to Cambridge or the Boston area." She then heads to the bathroom allowing me to get dressed and let myself out.

That was it.

I don't even know Suzie's last name, but I know her story—I've seen it before. If it's not an old man, it's a white man. Sisters are looking for a certain "lifestyle" that brothers their age, far too often, aren't providing or can't provide.

Decent brothers in their age group usually have other financial responsibilities. For example kids, and they usually have at least two children by age thirty. If they were lucky enough to go to college, they have student loans. If they aren't riding the bus, they have a car payment with expensive car insurance. If they have all of this going on, they don't own a home yet. How can they? There's no room to save for a down payment. They are either living with their mother or have a roommate. If that's not the case, then they are renting an over-priced apartment in an urban area. These types of brothers aren't even on the radar of the Sexy Suzie's of the world. The Sexy Suzie's of the world want to be taken care of. They want access. They want the overpriced things in life and they'll sacrifice the possibility of something powerful like Black Love in exchange for an opulent lifestyle.

Peter:

I have to see my PO today. I really don't know why I have to be on probation and pay a fee. It makes no sense to me. I'm on probation because I got caught distributing. I was distributing because the child support mafia is out to get me. The job that I was working at the time wasn't paying me enough to pay rent, child support and eat. The only good thing was that the lease was in my girlfriend Crystal's name. If I was short she'd have to make up the difference, not me. I ventured into the distribution game and got caught up—the shit we do to make ends meet.

Now, here I am, on my way to check in with my PO and pay a fee. What is the fee for anyway? What is it paying for? I must be supplementing the probation departments salary—I don't see what else this fee is paying for. I get salty every time I go there. To say that I have a bad attitude is putting it lightly. A grown ass man shouldn't have to check in with anyone, especially a woman. My PO's attitude could use some adjusting too. She gets on my fucking nerves.

"Peter you're late," she says barely looking up at me. I can't stand her bossy ass. She has an opened bag of Doritos on her desk. She punches some keys on her computer and then organizes some documents on her desk. I notice that her right thumb, index and middle finger have a cheese stain on them. She notices too. This nasty broad licks her fingers. I don't respond to her immediately. This chic is going to have to acknowledge me by looking me in my eyes. When she doesn't hear my response she looks up at me with a look of irritation.

"I'm here," I say blandly. I can tell she doesn't like my nonchalant response, but I don't give a fuck.

"Listen, today is not the day. I'm tired of you coming in here sulking because you're on probation. Over here acting like I caught the case and I am supposed to be answering to you. Let me remind you that you're the one here because you don't know how to act right. You're lucky your behind ain't locked up."

Fucking bitch, I think to myself.

"Can I go? I don't have any updates for you. I paid my fee. I got stuff to do," I say with base in my voice. She looks at me as if I've lost my mind.

"All you gotta do is show up, pay your fee, and stay out of trouble. If you weren't out here poisoning our people so that you could make a profit you wouldn't have to do this. So, shut up and sit there while I do my paperwork. You try to leave and I'll surrender you."

"Surrender me for what? I didn't do anything!" I say a little too loud for her liking.

"You better lower your motherfucking mouth when you're in my office." She says with a stereotypical black girl attitude. I think I saw her neck move a little bit too. She continues.

"You know what is bittersweet about what's going on right here? I'm going to always have a job because there are always going to be sorry ass dudes like you that don't know how to take care of themselves. You think you can sell a few drugs and that will solve all your problems. Dudes like you don't see far enough to look at the bigger picture. You want that quick fix money, but you don't want to accept responsibility when you get caught. That victim mentality you hold on to is not a good look."

"Are you my mother or my P.O.?" I'm heated. She can see that it's taking all that I have not go off on her. She picks up her bag of Doritos and starts eating them shits in front of me like she's watching a sitcom. She licks her fingers again. I wonder if she washes her hands after she pees or if she just licks them. She then comes from behind her desk and walks over to the brown cabinet next to the door. When she opens the cabinet door it's full of piss cups.

"You're talking kinda crazy to me today. Are you high? I think you're high… Here." She says with bass in her voice and then hands me a plastic cup.

"What's this for?"

"I'm giving you something else to complain about. Now add drug testing to your woes."

Nappy headed bitch. "You know that's not right. You can't do that shit!" I yell.

"I can and I will. So, take you whiney ass to the bathroom down the far end of the hall. A male PO will meet you there to unlock the door and monitor you. See you in two weeks. Sooner if your urine comes back dirty, nig—,"she says slamming the door behind me. *Did she just call me a Nigger?*

A few moments later, I walk out of the courthouse heated. It's funny that she called me a nigger but she's the one with the nigger naps. These so called "natural" sisters done let their hair go and think that shit looks cute. That shit looks crazy to me. I don't know how she is working in a professional establishment looking like that. Black women wonder why nobody wants them. How does she expect for people to show her respect if it looks like she doesn't respect herself? She needs to do something with that head. I'm not a fan of braids, but anything is better than what her hair is doing. She should really look into that. Nobody wants a nappy headed chick when they have access to perms, wigs and weaves. Maybe then, some man might pay her a little attention.

She'd lighten up a little if she got fucked once in a while. She needs to ease up on a brother. If she tames that head of hers, I might do some community service and give her a mercy fuck. She's a little thick for my liking but if it would get me some privileges while on probation, I'll hit her off. No problem.

3

JIM CROW BLUES

Elijah:

I'm in line at the Market Basket in Salem. The only reason why I'm here is because I got some work this morning outside of Home Depot. The dude that hired a group of us for the day was cool. He brought us all back to the Home Depot parking lot after our day was over. I say he was cool because he didn't have to do that. Most of the time when I do these day jobs, I have to find my way back. Fortunately, and unfortunately, I don't have a home to go back to. As long as there is a train station or a bus stop that leads to a train station, my home is wherever I'm at for that night.

I feel tired, but I feel good. I made seventy-five tax free dollars today. I walk pass Shaw's and decided to spend my hard-earned dollars where they'll go farther. Market Basket seems to always be packed. I pay no attention to the overflow of cars in the lot as I make my way to the entrance. Once inside, I locate my few items and head towards the registers.

Now, I'm in line with what feels like the entire city of Salem. I guess there's a big game coming on. If there's not a big game, there's a big storm. It makes no sense that I'm standing in a twelve-items or less line that extends down the cereal aisle. It took me two minutes to grab what I need, but it's taking me ten times that waiting in line to pay for it. I bet if everyone was asked to check their blood pressure before entering the store and then while they are there, they'd find that everyone's blood pressure would be elevated. I get stressed just walking in here.

It's as if someone read my mind and it only took them twenty minutes to read it. The other twelve items or less register opens. As I step up to head to the other register, I get cut off by a carriage. I don't smoke or drink, so my reflexes are on point. I step back before my foot gets run over. I then look at the man that cut me off in amazement. There's no way that he could say that he didn't see me. The way that he cuts me off is as if my 6 ft. 4 stature is invisible and he knows it. Yet, he doesn't even acknowledge that he did it. I hate that shit.

I size him up. My blood is boiling. If you're going to be gangster, be gangster with it all the way. Look me in my eye as if to say "yeah I cut you." He pulled some straight punk shit. The move that he pulled is equivalent to being in heavy traffic at an intersection. The cars that are perpendicular to you also have heavy slow-moving traffic. They know that they shouldn't block the intersection, but they still do. When the oncoming traffic's light changes to green, nobody can move. What does the person inside of the car do that is blocking traffic do? They look straight ahead like they can't see or hear the cars trying to get through the light.

That's what this man reminds me of. He's making a gangster move in a passive aggressive manner. I'm judging, but in this case, I feel like it's warranted. He looks like a baby boomer that misses segregation. He's elderly, Caucasian and ignorant. I tell myself to let it go, but I can't. The person behind me shakes their head when I look back at them as if to say "Did you see that shit?" I go behind the old man in line with my two items.

You think your white skin makes you superior to me? There's no way that I'm going to let this go.

"Sir, I'm not sure if you realized it, but you almost ran me over with your carriage." The cashier looks at me and then at him. He doesn't acknowledge me—just like those common courtesy violators that hold up traffic.

"Sir, did you hear me?" This time I say a little louder in case his old ass has a hearing problem.

The entire line should have heard me this time. He doesn't say anything. He just keeps looking at the cashier. I decide that he's a racist asshole. This isn't a battle that I need to fight in 2017. These Caucasians are taking off the masks that they had to wear during the Obama Administration. Now that Trump is in office folks are emboldened to show people just how they truly feel.

The cashier rings him up and hands him his receipt. He puts his stuff in the carriage and shuffles off. I pay for my items and notice that the old guy left one of his bags. I let the cashier know.

With a heavy Dominican accent she whispers in his direction, "Sir, you left your bag," then looks at me and laughs. She clearly doesn't care.

"If you want to go chase him that's up to you. I'd say it serves him right. Take his shit with you. Don't worry I won't say anything."

My conscience won't let me act like I didn't see him leave his bag. I know that if I hurry I can catch him. I finish pay for my items then rush out of Market Basket. I see him putting his bags into his green Camry. I yell over to him.

"Sir!" He doesn't look to see who is calling him. I yell to him again. "Sir, you left your bag!" He hurries into his minivan. When I almost get to his minivan, he slams the door and locks it as he sees me closely approaching. I know he sees me because we make eye contact. Purposely, ignoring me he backs out with reckless abandon. I just miss getting hit. That's two times he almost ran me over. My conscience is going to have to take the back seat today. I'm keeping his stuff.

I leave with his bag and head to Eastern bank. Never a dull moment at that place. I need to deposit the cash that I have left after my Market Basket experience. It's the end of the day. The bank is closing soon.

***

The teller at Eastern Bank greets me.

"I can take you over here."

She looks familiar. You know how it is when you know that you know someone, but you can't place where you know them from. I approach the counter.

"I'd like to make a deposit into my savings account."

"Do you have your slip, Sir?" She's looking at me with her kind and gentle familiar eyes.

"I'm sorry. I've had quite a day. I don't know where my heads at. Do you want me to get out of line and go to the front to fill one out?"

"No. That's fine Elijah. I'll fill it out for you. How much do you want to deposit?"

Did she just call me Elijah? "I'm sorry. I've been trying to figure out where I know you from. Now that you've said my name and I haven't given you my driver's license, it's evident that we know each other."

"I figured that you didn't recognize me. It's me, Silvie."

Damn she looks good. I sure didn't recognize her. When she shows up to the shelter she doesn't look like this. Don't get me wrong. You can tell that she's a good-looking woman when she volunteers at the shelter, but she is usually dressed down. She wears her hair pulled back in a bun. She doesn't wear any make up and she wears loose fitting clothes.

The woman that I am staring at right now is done up from head-to-toe. I can only see her from waist up, but I can't imagine that the bottom half doesn't look just as good. Now, I'm nervous and a little embarrassed. I don't look good at all. I can't even say that I look halfway decent. Today, I worked construction so my clothes are dirty and I'm sure she can smell me from behind the glass.

"Hi Silvie. How are you?" I say as I fight the urge to put my head down. This is not how I want her to see me. Even when I go to the shelter, I make sure that I look ok and that I don't stink. At this moment, I feel low. I feel bad for myself. I'm sure she's thinking "poor thing" or something along those lines.

"Honestly, I've been better. I can't complain though. I am healthy. I have a roof over my head… Did I just say that last part? I'm sorry Elijah."

"What do you have to be sorry about? Those are things that you should be grateful for. It's ok to say it." I know that she didn't mean to slight me. I try to make her feel ok about it. She's always been kind to me. I can't see her stopping today.

"Thanks. Here you are trying to comfort me and I'm the insensitive one. I really am sorry Elijah. Let me make it up to you," she says while completing the transaction.

"Make what up to me? I told you it's fine. You don't need to do anything for me," I say as she hands me my slip.

"Let me take you to dinner. I'm starving and you look like you had a hard day." Her cheeks flush with embarrassment. "Oops. Did I just say that?"

"You're on a roll," I say laughing.

"I don't know why I keep putting my foot into my mouth. I just figured that since I am going to get something to eat, it would be nice to have some company."

"As much as I'd love to, I can't. It was good seeing you though. You look very nice Silvie. Please, enjoy your meal, I'm sure I'll see you soon." I smile taking my slip and then I walk away towards the exit.

I leave the Salem branch and think about what just happened. Had I been in a different situation, a stable one, I would have taken her up on that dinner date. I don't want her first date with me to be one that she foots the bill for. She deserves better. I'm in no position to add any value to her life. Sometimes when I see her at the shelter, I hear her talk to another volunteer that she's friends with. I feel conflicted about eavesdropping but through those conversations I learn a little bit more about her. Silvie has a son by a man that doesn't seem to be doing his job as a dad. I don't have any kids, but I can't see anything that would be more important than making sure that my seed is taken care of. I decided to take myself out of the equation before any math is done. She's struggling herself. She doesn't need me adding to her struggle. I won't be that brother.

I walk up to the end of the plaza to wait for a bus on Highland Ave that's heading towards Lynn. I'll be hanging around there tonight. Hopefully, I can lay my head at the purple line with no problems. I can see the number 459 bus coming up the street. I run across the street to the opposite side to catch it. The bus driver sees me trying to cross and dodge traffic. He pulls over to the bus stop although nobody is waiting there and waits for me. Out of breath, I thank him and take a seat after paying my fare. I sit the bags next to me and remember the bag from the baby boomer. With all the running around I did, I haven't even looked inside of the bag that the racist jerk gifted me.

When I open the bag, I knew today was my day. He must have been doing his Christmas shopping in Market Basket. The first thing I notice is a battery-operated trimmer inside of the bag—just what I needed. It will come in handy for my public bathroom grooming. I dig through the bag some more and can't believe my eyes. I blink to make sure that I'm not seeing things. There are five gift cards at fifty dollars apiece in the bag. All five of them are American Express gift cards. God sure is an amazing God! To top it off there is a package of soft oatmeal cookies that cost ninety-nine cents a pack. I know this because they are one of the things I went in the store to buy for myself. Oatmeal cookies are my favorite. I notice a box of BIG Cheez-It's is on top of something. I move it to the side and see two greeting cards underneath. I open the cards. Both are birthday cards. Inside each of the cards are two five-dollar scratch tickets. I'm not sure how the scratch tickets got in there. He must have put them with the cards so that he wouldn't forget. I'm not a lottery type of guy. Nobody that you know really wins anyway. I don't have the slightest urge to scratch them so I put them back inside of the birthday cards. The bus ride to Lynn will be at least fifteen minutes. I decide to listen to "Mirror" by Lalah Hathaway on repeat the entire way. Today was a good day.

Shawn:

I will say that they were very discreet with their affair. I can't find any evidence of it. If I wasn't on the other side of the door when she was having the conversation that ruined my life, I might not have ever caught her. She would have been pregnant and I would have thought that it was my baby. I would have raised my best-friend's child. That's so messed up. I still haven't spoken to him. I don't know if I'll ever be ready to. Right now, I still want to do some serious damage to him.

How do you do that to your boy? I've always had his back. I've always looked out for him. I've even let him stay at my place when he was in between girlfriends. He never has a place of his own. He just bounces from female to female and lives with them. The last time that he stayed with me, I told him that he could stay with me until he got on his feet. I told him that he didn't have to pay rent, this way he could stack his money and save for the deposit on an apartment of his own.

Over time, I noticed that this dude was living well…too well to be saving money. He was going out all the time and he had collected a few women over a month's span. I wondered how much money he had saved towards his apartment. I was cooking dinner when he walked into the kitchen talking on his cell. When he finished his call he greeted me with a "What up?" I got straight to the point.

"Peter, how much money do you have saved towards your apartment?"

"Damn Shawn, Why are you all in my business? You sound like one of my baby mamas asking about my pockets."

"Watch your mouth brother," I said with a look of seriousness on my face.

"Nah yo, I'm just saying. Why are you sweating me about my money? You told me that I could stay here for free until I get on my feet. Well, that's what I'm trying to do. I'll be outta here soon enough. I've been dealing with this white girl for the past few weeks. The way I've estimated things, I will be out of here within the next two weeks," he said.

"The point was for you to save enough money to get your own place. I wanted you to not have to depend on a woman for your place of residence. You'll always be in the same position if you keep doing the same thing. As soon as you get tired of her or fired by her, you'll need to find a new place. Aren't you tired of this life?"

"Shawn you sound crazy. I don't get fired. I leave."

"Just like all these jobs you've had, right Peter?"

"On that note, I'll be outta here in a week. I'm not gonna stay here and have you thinking you can talk to me any old kind of way!"

That was the last time Peter stayed at my place. It was hard for me to stop trying to get him to see the big picture, but I couldn't do it any longer. He's my friend, but he isn't my son. I don't have a responsibility to him, at least not on that level. If he wants to keep living his life this way, so be it. That's his business. I decided three years ago that I would no longer make it mine.

Here I am today trying to figure out how in hell he could betray me the way that he did. We've been boys since childhood so I considered him family. You just don't treat your family like that. He lived with me from eighth grade to the tenth grade. After that point he went back home to live with his mom. I'll never forget the night that he came to my house. The landline phone rung and both my mother and I answered it at the same time. I was about to hang up once my mom said hello, but the voice on the other line was unfamiliar and I was nosey.

"Hello, this is Amy Jefferson from the Department of Social Services. May I speak to Shawna Carson please."

"This is she. What can I do for you?"

"Hello, Ms. Carson."

"*Mrs.* Carson thank you."

"Oh, I'm sorry. Hello, Mrs. Carson. Are you familiar with The Jones family? I was told that I could call you to see if Peter Jones could stay with you."

"Stay with me? What's wrong with where he's at? Where's his mom?"

"I'm sorry Mrs. Carson. There's been an incident at the Jones home and Peter will be placed in foster care if you aren't able to take him into your home for the night. We will go to court tomorrow and talk about a more permanent placement, but for tonight he either goes with you or with us."

"Well what the hell happened?"

"There's been a report of sexual abuse. We need him removed from the home while we investigate."

"Well, where is his sister? Doesn't she need a place to stay too?"

"Um, Mrs. Carson we are investigating the sister. They need to be separated."

"Oh my God! Yes. Sure. Bring him here. He can stay here until things get figured out."

I couldn't believe what I just heard. A sexual assault happened...between Peter and his *sister*....

I immediately went to my mom and confessed that I listened to the call. I told her that I wasn't sure if I was comfortable with him coming to live with us if he forced himself on his own sister. My mom sat me down and told me that it wasn't my decision. She punished me for listening to a grown folks' conversation and told me to make sure that my upper bunk bed had clean sheets. Peter would be living with us. I later learned from "listening to grown folks' conversations" that Peter didn't rape his sister—she raped him. She got to stay at home and he stayed with us.

Two years later, his sister went off to a college out of state. Peter was allowed to move back home as long as his mom promised to not have her daughter back in the home. That didn't last long. When a school break occurred, his sister was back in the home. As soon as I found out, I told my mom. She called Ms. Jones and mentioned her concerns to Peter's mom. From what I could tell from my mother's tone and facial expressions, Peter's mom was going off on her. Peter stayed home and would only come to my house from time to time; usually when he'd get into big fights with his mom. He never gave any specifics. I respected his privacy.

This same man slept with my fiancée. Thinking back, that's a lot more I can say for the social worker that told my mom all the Jones Family's business. Aren't their limits to what they can and can't disclose?

Jean:

I have to fly out of town this morning for a dinner meeting in Maryland. Since it was a last-minute thing, I have crappy seats on the flight—middle seats in the back of the plane. As I've gotten older, I've noticed that I've been getting motion sickness more often. If I'm in the back seat of a small car, I get nauseous. If I'm in the back row of a small plane, I start to get hot, real hot, like I need to strip down right this minute hot. Minutes later nausea always creeps in.

I only have a carry-on bag since I'm traveling for one night. The light skin flight attendant starts announcing zones. She looks like my lying ass ex. She probably has color issues too. She was probably raised by a family full of house niggers that were brainwashed—a family conditioned to think that the closer they get to looking like their superior, the closer they get to attaining the status of their superior. I feel bad for her. She probably doesn't know that white America still sees her as nigger.

She probably wouldn't give me any play. Women like her come from families that keep their complexions uniform by not having kids with anyone any darker than them. That's how my ex's family got down. This flight attendant is triggering all types of unwanted memories.

I don't usually travel on Jet Blue, American Airlines is my preference. They separate you into groups for boarding. Due to my miles, I am always in group four. That is the group that is called right after first class. I've gotten accustomed to boarding before the masses.

To my surprise, I get to board first because my seat is all the way in the back. Jet Blue boards in the reverse. Wow! An airline doing something that makes sense. I know that I'm only feeling their boarding process because it benefits me today. Otherwise, if my seats were in the front, I'd be swearing and complaining about how it makes no sense having to wait until the end.

I find my seat and I don't bother to buckle up. I know that I'm going to have to move as soon as the person comes that is sitting at the window seat. I'm ready to get comfortably situated, as comfortable as you can in a middle seat. So far, it is just me and this Asian dude in our row. I'm feeling optimistic. It's looking like the person that is supposed to be in the window seat isn't going to make this flight. The last person gets on the flight. It's a white woman with an infant.

I'm silently praying that she doesn't sit down near me. For many reasons, the last person that I want to sit next to is a white woman breast feeding her infant. To my luck, my prayers are answered. She sits down a few rows ahead of me. *Great.* I move myself over to the window seat. I fasten my seat belt and pull out a book I've been wanting to read but haven't had the time. Just as I am about to put my headphones into my ear, I feel a presence watching me.

Shit.

"Hi. I think that you are in my seat," he says with a typical Seven Eleven accent.

"My bad bro. I thought everyone boarded the plane. I'm in the middle seat." The person in the aisle seat gets up to let me out and Seven Eleven in.

"Thank you both," he says and then sits in his seat.

When I sit back down, I feel like I am about to vomit. The plane hasn't even started to move and I have motion sickness. *What the hell is that smell?* I scream inside of my head. My nostrils are flared. My face looks distorted. I can't see myself, but I can feel my facial muscles flexing. I swear to God it smells like I'm on a bus in Barbados where nobody uses deodorant as a daily hygiene item. The person next to me is not from Barbados. At least he doesn't look like it. I guess the bus I'm on is in India.

This funky ass dude doesn't smell like he forgot to put on his deodorant today. No. He smells like he never put deodorant on a day in his life. The flight is full. There is nowhere for me to move my seat to. I'm dying. The plane hasn't even pulled out yet and I'm feeling like shit. This man smells so bad that I think I'm going to stink because I am sitting next to him. I look to my right wondering if the guy next to me has the same reaction, only to be equally disgusted. *Did Asian dude just pick his nose and flick it?*

I guess technically they are both Asian. The ignorant asshole inside of me wants to tell both these dudes about their nasty asses. More specifically, I want to tell the man in the window seat to take his behind to the bathroom and wash up as much as he can, but I don't. With my luck Seven Eleven is a physician and I might need him to save my life on this flight. I'm not going to burn any potential bridges. I can't help it though. The stink permeating from his body is unbearable. I can't breathe. He has my oxygen in a choke hold and there's not much that I can do. I'm trapped. I cover my nose and mouth with my hand. If I don't vomit all over these men in my row, it will be a miracle.

As I try to decide whether I should breathe through my nose or just my mouth, I pick up my reading material for the flight, *Animal* by K'wan. I saw this brother on an

Iceberg Slim documentary. I haven't read all his books, but the ones that I have read have all been bangers. Speaking of Iceberg Slim, that reminds me of a line from his book, *Pimp*:

"I smelled the stink that only a street whore has after a long, busy night."

Imagine that smell. That smell doesn't have anything on Seven Eleven over here. The hour and a half long flight into Maryland felt like a five-hour flight. I managed, by the grace of God, to keep all my stomach acids from seeping out of my mouth. I was nauseous the entire flight. I couldn't even read my book. I had to keep my eyes shut and strategically take sips of air. I try to think of ways to prevent this from happening again. There's no way you can choose who sits beside you when you're on a plane. I could get a first-class flight and that would filter out all the broke people. Income level has nothing to do with if you stink or not, unless you're homeless. That's an entirely different conversation.

There's no need to rush to get a spot in the aisle. I'd be standing for fifteen minutes if I did. I decide to people watch. It never fails. Somebody always bumps their head trying to rush. Another person always bangs their bag into someone while taking it down from the overhead compartment. And you can always count on someone from the front that put their bag towards the back to go against traffic. I get to watch it all unfold from the comfort of my last row middle seat with Seven Eleven. Meanwhile, he's huffing and puffing because the Asian dude in the aisle seat got up to stand in the aisle, but I didn't. I haven't even taken off my seatbelt. I know I'm irritating Seven Eleven, but I'm in no rush. He didn't think about how I was going to survive his funk. I could care less if he wants me to contort my body to appear as though I'm attempting to deplane. I dare him to say something.

Elijah:

"Hello Elijah," a smiling face greets me.

"Hello," I say smiling even harder. She has her hair done differently today. It's pulled back, but she has bangs today. She also has on fitted jeans and a black V-neck t-shirt that says "Genetically Resilient" in red lettering. I need one of those. I haven't bought anything for myself except necessities, but I'm going to make an exception for this shirt. I'll remember to ask her where she got it from before we leave.

I head to the line to get a hot meal. Lately, the shelter is becoming more crowded. With the weather changing people want to be indoors. It is staying colder longer, which equates to more bodies in here. The line to get some food is long as hell, but I really don't have anywhere to be.

As I find my position in line, I check out what they have on the menu. I hear my name again.

"Elijah!" Silvie is waving for me to come over. I don't want to lose my spot in line; I could risk not getting a full meal and having to settle with what's left. Usually what's left is not much of anything. Despite my reluctance, I get out of line to see what Silvie needs. As I approach her, I notice the way she chews gum. She chews with her mouth open. It makes her even cuter.

"Elijah, we saved you a plate. We knew that you wouldn't beat the rush and didn't want you to go hungry, then have the nerve to let you help us clean up after everyone later. So, here you go." She hands me a plate wrapped in tinfoil. I notice that she kept saying we, but I know she was talking about herself.

"Ah man, you didn't have to do that but thank you. I don't expect any special treatment. In my house, I was taught that if a woman takes the time to feed you, it is your responsibility to make sure to eat all of it and clean up after. So, the way I see it, all of you women are cooking for us. We should be helping out, with the clean-up. But like I said, thank you. I truly appreciate your thoughtfulness."

"Ok, I'll let you enjoy your meal. I guess I'll see you later on," she says smiling. Silvie has a beautiful smile.

"Ok," I say and head over to table near the far corner of the cafeteria. I smile to myself. She didn't correct me when I said, "your thoughtfulness". She took the credit. I knew it was her doing and not everyone's. *Another place, another time.*

I find a seat and start eating. There's mac and cheese, baked chicken and collard greens. It's pretty good too. When I see the dessert I almost put it to the side. The only reason I don't is because I see her watching me. I wonder why she keeps grilling me from the serving table. I'm not a big fan of apple pie; I'm more of a sweet potato pie man. Silvie is staring and I have a feeling it's because of this pie. I don't want to be disrespectful so I eat the apple pie. I scrape the vanilla ice cream off the pie and eat it as if it's the best pie ever. Had I been more of a paranoid person, I would have thought that someone poisoned my food the way that she was looking at me. I later find out that Silvie made the pie. One of the other ladies told Silvie that "she put her foot in it."

The cafeteria is in shutdown mode. The women are cleaning and I'm doing the heavy lifting. I actually look forward to this. I feel useful. They truly appreciate me being there to help, I know this for a fact. One Saturday, I didn't show up to eat. The next time that I came, they all cussed me out for not letting them know that I wouldn't be coming to work that day. They laughed about it, but I know they felt my absence. They had to move all the chairs and tables themselves. I'm sure it took them and extra hour to get out of there and go home.

Since then, I treat this like a part-time job and show up to help the ladies out. They are truly a great bunch of women. All of them, except for one, are single. I know this because I get to hear bits and pieces of their conversations as I am moving things. The stuff that I hear I could write a book about. It's hilarious! Being here makes me forget about my situation. That is until I look at Silvie and wish that I was in a different position. If I wasn't homeless, I would have stepped to her a long time ago.

I finish my chores and head out. I say my goodbye's— although Silvie and I don't speak—and walk out of the building. I usually wait in the parking lot out of plain sight to make sure Silvie gets into her car ok. She doesn't know that I do this. I, honestly don't want her to know. I don't want to spook her. She might take it the wrong way and think I'm stalking her.

I hear the way that the other men talk about the volunteers during meal time. It's downright scary. It sounds like there are a few rapists in the mix. I just want to make sure that Silvie gets home in one piece. The last thing a woman needs when she leaves her home to volunteer and help the homeless is to get sexually assaulted by the same man she fed.

Silvie usually sits in her car for a while before taking off. Today is no different. She doesn't even start it. She just sits. I'm not sure if she is meditating or praying. I can't tell from where I am standing. All the other volunteers leave the parking lot before she does. After the last of the volunteers leave, Silvie starts her car. The sound that I hear coming from her car tells me that she is not going anywhere at the time being. I head over to her car to help.

"Sounds like your car is mad at you." Silvie smiles at me.

"It sure does. I've called Triple A. They said that they should be here in an hour," Silvie says while shaking her head.

"An hour? I thought that they were quicker than that."

"Elijah, I don't know if you have any plans, but I sure would appreciate it if you sat here with me until they came. Then I could drive you to wherever you are going after," She unlocks her passenger side door. I hesitate before getting in. I decide to stop thinking so hard about this situation and let it just happen.

It smells like cinnamon in her car. She has "This Love" by India Arie playing on her phone. I'd be saving my battery life instead of listening to music, but I don't say anything.

An hour and a half later into our conversation I mention that Triple A hasn't made it here yet nor have they called.

"I wasn't expecting them," she says with a devious look on her usually angelic face.

"What's that supposed to mean?" I ask.

"Well, Elijah, I've never experienced a homeless man playing hard to get. So, I did what any normal girl would do. I set you up. I'm actually pretty handy when it comes to cars. My car not being able to start was done deliberately. I know that you regularly watch to make sure that I get to my car safely."

She really caught me off guard. This entire time she knew. Silvie is something else. I start to chuckle to myself.

"You mean to tell me that nothing is wrong with your car and you knew that I'd come out of hiding to check on you. You were plotting?" I say with a playful look of being appalled by her gestures.

"Yup," she says cut and dry.

"How'd you know that I'd take the bait?" Now I'm intrigued.

"I knew because I know that you like me. You just won't let yourself tell me. You didn't have to tell me though. It shows through your actions. Am I sorry for setting you up? Nope. I had one more tactic up my sleeve to get you alone if this didn't work. Next, I was going to change my shirt in the car knowing that you'd be watching. When I would have lifted my shirt, you'd see your name written across my two breasts. If I had to go that far and it didn't work I don't know what I would have tried next," Silvie says cracking up. *I love her smile.*

"Thank God you didn't have to strip to get me to talk to you," I say laughing with her. *This feels good.* Then she shocks the shit out of me. She leans over and kisses me; not on the cheek but right on the lips. She thanks me for routinely looking out for her and for being such a kind, compassionate, generous, giving man. She said she knows men with way more in life that give so much less.

"Where to Mr. Elijah?"

"The closest Planet Fitness." She looks at me strange.

"Planet Fitness. You're going to work out now? Ok, are you homeless or not?"

I laugh. "No, I am very homeless and I maintain my gym membership, that way I am able to keep up with my hygiene. I work-out for a little while and then use their shower to get the days grime off me. It's worth the $20 a month membership."

"Aren't you resourceful. You definitely don't fit the stereotype of what homeless looks like. I can't say that I've ever wanted to kiss a homeless man but I don't regret it. That explains why your lips weren't hard and ashy."

"You thought my lips were going to be hard and ashy and you still kissed me?" I ask playfully.

"Yup. You know today is Thirsty Thursday!" She says cracking herself up. Then she continues. "I have to go to Malden Station. Is it ok if I bring you there first? Then I can bring you to the gym."

"Malden Station is cool. I know that place well. I'll get out there and walk to Planet Fitness," I say.

We continue getting to know each other during the thirty-minute drive to Malden Station. When we arrive, she pulls her black Honda Accord up to the drop off area. As I begin to get out I thank her for the interesting day. She stops me before I get out and kisses me again. I feel her inviting her tongue into my mouth while the heat of her hand rest on my zipper. I try to stop my penis from jumping up and giving her hand a dap, but it does anyway. She stops kissing me.

"I just wanted to make sure the connection that I felt to you was mutual. And judging from what I just felt in my hand, you feel the connection," she says grinning.

I get out of the car with my head spinning. I forgot to ask her where she got her shirt from. I prepare myself for the walk-through Malden Square down to the Planet Fitness on Eastern Ave. It's a long walk, but I have a lot of thoughts to sift through on the way. I can't say that I would have imagined my day would have gone this way but I have no complaints. None at all.

Peter:

I told Silvie if she wanted the child support money that I give her, she was going to have to come to my job and get it. That's exactly what she did. What I wasn't expecting was to see some dude getting out of her car. I know that she dates folks, but why is she bringing them with her to pick up money from me? To my surprise, he got out of the car before I made my way over. This dude looks mad familiar to me. I can't remember where I've seen him before. I need to stop smoking so much weed; my memory might be a little better. I get to her car.

"Who was that dude that got out of your car?" I ask as if I'm still her man.

"Mind your business Peter," she says with that same black girl attitude that my P.O. has.

"You need money from me, not the other way around. Remember that shit the next time you open your mouth to get smart with me," I yell. I don't know why I'm yelling but I'm pissed. I like that I'm standing outside of her driver's side door looking down on her as we make this exchange. I like that she has to look up to me as she speaks.

"Are you giving me the money for YOUR SON or not. I don't have time for this drama."

"Drama? That's what you call this? Drama. This ain't drama. This is you leaving one man to go ask money from another. Why didn't you get money from the dude that just left your car? Did he just leave your bed too? I know he did, because I know how you get down. It doesn't take long to get inside those panties."

"Keep your disgusting comments to yourself. I just came here for the money. Do you have it or not? I have to go pick up YOUR SON from his uncle's house and you're making me late."

"I ain't seen that bougie, black panther party member in a minute. He's a funny motherfucker! Tell that nigga I said what's up," I say sarcastically. She looks at me like she didn't hear a word that I just said.

"Here," I throw the envelope on the passenger seat— the same seat that dude she had in the car was sitting on.

"The next time you come to collect money from me don't have no dude with you or else I'm not giving it to you. You can get whatever you need for 'my son' from him, since he is getting what you said was 'my' pussy."

She snatches the money and puts it into her pocket book. She then rolls up the passenger side window. She doesn't say goodbye. She just drives off.

Bitch.

I can't front. She still looks good. If she let me, I'd be all up in those panties again. Patrice still lets me hit it from time to time. Not Silvie. She shut that shit down once she found out about Patrice. I tried to hit it a few times over the years. I've even offered to pay her an extra $25 every two weeks in her child support check if she let me hit it. The bitch had the nerve to laugh at me. She laughed like she didn't used to suck this dick. She laughed like she forgot who gave her multiple orgasms. She's fronting, but she knows what's up.

Speaking of what's up, Shawn finally came out of his depression and hit me up. He told me that he never found out who slept with her and at this point he doesn't even care. I invited him out, but he said he wasn't ready yet. He still had some self-reflecting or some shit to do. I forget the phrase he used. What it amounts to is that he's not ready to get back into the dating scene. I told him just because he had his heart broken, doesn't mean his penis had to act disabled too. He needs to get back in these streets. Some pussy will help him forget about the pussy he never got.

I feel his pain though. He spent a lot of time, energy and money on pussy that he never got a chance to taste. I didn't do anything except feed that same pussy some game and then this dick. I tried to tell this nigga that bitches ain't shit. I'll wait on him to come around and give him his time. I'm glad he hit me up though. I've missed my homie.

Shawn:

I called Peter. He has no clue that I know it was him that impregnated my fiancé. I'm glad. He's going to get his. Karma will knock on his door soon enough. I'm going to be right there when she does. I got something for Nakia too. They both think that they can play me and get off with no consequences. They're bugging. It's on.

I'm going to start with Nakia. Since she likes to keep secrets from me, I'm going to start leaking the secrets that she told me. When you're in a relationship, the secrets your friends and family members share never stop with the person they are disclosing it to. If they are in a serious relationship, you must know that the secrets extend to the person they are in a relationship with. So, if you tell Jane that you can't stand your boss, you better believe that you are telling Jane and her man John.

My first stop will be to "coincidentally" run into Thomas. He is the boyfriend of Nakia's best friend, Tiffany. I know that he likes to go to the Silver Slipper in Roxbury for breakfast on Saturday mornings. I know this because Tiffany and Nakia get their hair done every Saturday morning at Styllistik Hair Salon in Dorchester. Thomas drops Tiffany off, then gets his breakfast at the Silver Slipper while she's at the salon. He is there so often that he's considered a regular. He sits there for hours socializing.

If Tiffany isn't done by the time he's ready to leave, he heads down to Washington Street and stops by the Black Market. I've heard great things about the place. There are always unique finds in there. I think that most of the vendors in there are black, hence the name Black Market, but I don't know for sure.

I have a taste for some grits and eggs. Today is Saturday. I decide to drive over to the Silver Slipper and say what's up to Thomas.

***

"Yo, Shawn! What's good?" Thomas yells over to me.

"Hey, Thomas. Long time no see," I say to him as he gives me a hug.

"Come sit down at my table. What you been up to?" He asks while stuffing a piece of bacon into his mouth.

"I've been ok. I've been just going to work, going to the gym and trying to get my mind right. What about you? What have you been up to?"

"Oh, you know. I been just letting myself get bossed around by my girl because that's how relationships work according to Tiffany," he says sarcastically and then laughs.

"Well, I let Nakia boss me around and that shit still didn't work out," I say laughing a little. I feel bad that I have to hurt Thomas just to hurt Nakia but fuck it. It's worth it. Like I said before, if one knows, so does the other. Tiffany knew. I'm sure that Thomas knew too.

"I just can't seem to find it in my heart to forgive her." *There's the bait. Now bite.*

"Yeah man, I know that was a lot and on your wedding day too!" He says and shakes his head.

"Yup. I'll never forget that. I don't know if I'll ever forgive Nakia for that. How did you forgive Tiffany for what she did to you?" *And there it is. No turning back now.*

"How did I forgive Tiffany for what?" He asks with an irritated tone.

"You know, how did you forgive her when she stepped out on you?"

"Are you sure you aren't mixing me up with somebody else? Maybe one of Nakia's other friends..."

"Nah, man. I am almost positive that I am talking about Tiffany. Nakia told me that she had a fling with her boss and you guys were going to couple's therapy to deal with it."

"Well, you know more than me. And we've never did any couple's counseling because I didn't know that we needed any." He fails at trying not to sound defensive.

"Yo, man. I'm sorry. I had no idea that you didn't know." I say to him. "The only thing that I know is that she slept with her boss. I don't know details…."

For a few moments he says nothing and there is an awkward moment of silence. I feel bad for him but my plan is going exactly how I imagined. The silence must be too much to bear.

"I'm gonna go to the Black market? You wanna roll with me?" He asks. We leave the conversation where it is.

"Sure, I heard that is where they sell the Genetically Resilient hoodies. I gotta get one of them."

"If what you said earlier is true, I think I'm gonna need one too," he says in a defeated tone.

"Ok, well, let me just get my bacon, egg and cheese sandwich to go." Reminding him that I came here to eat. I forget all about the grits.

"Aight, bet."

He sits at the table in silence waiting for me. His demeanor has changed. His spirit has changed. Even his posture has changed. I know exactly how he is feeling. And I know that he is going to investigate this and/or confront Tiffany. He knows if I know, I heard it from Nakia. Tiffany and Nakia are as thick as thieves and if Nakia told me, it's because Tiffany told her. I guess the saying is true. Birds of a feather *do* flock together.

We arrive at the Black Market. I feel good as soon as I walk through the door. I'm blown away by how nice it is. Black people and things made by black people—it's like a little city you'd find in Wakanda. This attractive light skin lady with braces wearing a beautiful African print head wrap greets Thomas and I. She asks me to sign in using my email address. She doesn't ask Thomas. I figure it is because he's been here before.

I feel my foot tapping involuntarily to the music being played by DJ Chris. I only know his name, because I see the flyer next to the sign in sheet. I could come here just for the music alone. I look around and I see of a roomful of black and brown people. It is a majestic sight. There is so much to look at. Each vendor has their section set up as if it is their little store. There is African art being sold, African clothing, African jewelry, beaded jewelry, natural hair care products, sunglasses, tee shirts with strong quotes on them and books.

I notice a vendor that has a *Bitter* hoodie on. I laugh because I can think of a few people I should give that to, myself included. When I look closer I realize that the vendor is selling books. Intrigued by her merchandising, I walk over to her table. She has three books that all have the word "Bitter" in the title. All the books are black with white lettering, each wrapped as a gift in red satin ribbon. She is wearing these futuristic glasses that are like an electronic billboard. The words VICKBREEDY.COM pop up across the lenses of the glasses. *Dope.*

I look to her left and there they are. I see what I came to the Black Market for. I'm confused because she has *Bitter* books with Genetically Resilient apparel. So, I ask her.

"Are you the author?"

"Yes, I'm Vick Breedy," she says with a huge smile. Her curly blonde hair that she wears natural stands out. It's as bright as her smile. As we talk I notice she's actually looking down on me. I hope she has on heels because I'm almost 6 feet and she's about two inches taller than me.

"So, I have two questions. What's up with these Bitter books and how are the Genetically Resilient hoodies related?

"I'm glad you asked."

I'm a little distracted because she has a laptop on the table playing a video that has some serious action going on. She notices my attention is divided.

"What you're watching are the book trailers for the entire *Bitter Series*."

"Wow! You got mini-movies with each book. That's impressive."

"The goal is to get make *Bitter* a movie. The kind of movie that you see on the big screen."

"Word? Well more power to you. You seem like the type of individual that is serious about her craft. I don't doubt that you'll make it a movie. Ok so tell me more about the correlations between your books and apparel."

"All three of my books are fiction. They are about the challenges we face within our relationships, friendships and family. One character remains bitter throughout the series. The books don't advocate for you to be bitter. They show you what happens to you when you remain bitter."

I know more than a few bitter people.

"That's good to know. I'll admit I assumed the opposite," I say.

"The Genetically Resilient apparel is for those that have bounce back magic. I actually use that as a hashtag. It's for anyone that has gone through something and bounced back from it. It represents my journey. I went through a few difficult periods in my life, just as the characters in my book did. I wrote a book as a response to the adversity that I faced instead of letting it take me out or keep me stuck. I tapped into my bounce back magic. Because I did that, I'm here talking to you about my trilogy and my apparel, when my story would have been very different had I not been resilient."

"Well damn. Let me get all three books and two Genetically Resilient hoodies. Do you take credit?"

As she is getting my purchases together I feel my foot tapping again, it's as if it has a life of its own. I have to make sure I give that DJ Chris dude a dap on the way out. He's playing all the jams. I take my purchases and Vick Breedy's business card. I wonder if that is her real name. She doesn't look like a Vick.

I look around the place to see where Thomas is. He's at a table where they are selling African backpacks and bags. He seems to be more interested in the shapely dreadlocked sister than what she's selling. I can't say that I blame him. I get his attention to let him know that I'm heading out. He pounds his heart two times with his fist. That serves as his goodbye and a thank you. I walk down Washington street to get to my car. When I get inside, I sit for a minute and think about what I just did. Tiffany will take her anger out on Nakia when she feels the heat from Thomas. I lost my best friend because of Nakia, now, she will lose her best friend for sharing a secret with me. I'm not stopping with that. She got some more to lose before I'm done. No regrets.

Peter:

I hear sirens just as I approach the end of the Commons in Lynn. I was just minding my motherfucking business, feeling good, jamming to a classic Biggie mix. As soon as I hear the sirens, I tense up and get that uneasy feeling that starts in your gut and shoots up to your throat. I'm trying to think of what I did. Was I speeding? Probably. I was just keeping up with the traffic. If I was speeding, it was no more than the person in front of me and beside me. I pull over and pray that they go past me and they aren't pulling me over. My anxiety is high right now. All this shit going on with racist cops killing black men on camera and getting away with it has got me shook. Being black is illegal. These motherfuckers pull me over and ignore all the others that were doing the same speed. I can literally feel my blood pressure raise.

Nowadays cops pull you over and you don't know if you're going to make it home to complain about it. These motherfuckers can shoot you while you're filming it and still get away with it—and they know it! I try to brace myself for the bullshit that is about to go down. I know that they are going to fuck with me. I just have to stay calm, keep both hands on the wheel and do what they say.

Both cops get out of the car. One comes to my window and the other goes to the passenger side looking through my windows. My driver's side window was already down. I was enjoying the breeze against my face.

"License and registration," the cop says without telling me what I'm being pulled over for.

"I'm going inside of my pocket for my wallet to get my license and then I gotta go inside of the glove compartment for the registration Officer," I say. I know I sound ridiculous, but I don't want to give these pigs any reason to think that I am about to pull out a weapon. I'm not trying to be included in their "killed another nigger" stats. FUCK that shit!

"Why are you speaking to me like I'm a fucking retard or are you the retard? Do I look slow to you? Get your fucking license and registration before I lock your ass up. Don't act like this is the first time you've been pulled over," he spits out.

I'm ready to go the fuck off on this cop. How does he know if I've been pulled over before or not? He hasn't even run anything yet.

I hand him my license and then I reach for my registration in the glove compartment. Just as I'm about to open the compartment, the second officer bangs the back window with his night stick. He scared the shit out of me.

"Go slow my brotha," he says with a smirk on his face. He's amused that he scared me more than I already was. I feel so fucking powerless and vulnerable. I hand the retarded cop my registration. Then my heart starts beating fast. I meant to pay the renewal for my registration and got caught up. I never did. I just gave them permission to really fuck with me now.

"You just sit tight Scooby Doo."

Did he just call me the cartoon dog Scooby Doo? I'm panicking. All white boys aren't racist, but these two are. I know my shit has expired. I don't realize it, but I'm holding my breath the entire time. They were only gone two minutes. The two cops come back to my car laughing as if they are telling jokes at my expense. If they arrest me, I'll be violating my probation. That gives my angry black woman probation officer the right to surrender me and I'll have to finish my time. There's no way I'm going jail. Not today!

"So, Peter, it looks like you are driving with an expired registration. Why is that? And your breath smells like you've been drinking. Have you been drinking?" The other officer chimes in.

"I don't know if he's been drinking, but the car smells like he's been using joints as air freshener," the first one adds. They both laugh. *These motherfuckers got jokes.*

"I have not been drinking Officer and I have not been smoking," I say. Only part of the statement is a lie. I was definitely smoking.

"Get out of the vehicle." The one on the driver's side yells. He's a young white boy with a red buzz cut. I can tell he works out because he's filling out his uniform like the Hulk.

Now my heart is pounding. This is how shit can go downhill fast. They're not going to find any drugs in my car unless they plant it. Why are these assholes fucking with me? Just give me a fine for driving with an expired registration and go harass somebody else. I guess I'm taking too long to get out of the car.

"Get out of the fucking car, you fucking monkey!"

I'd rather he call me a nigger. First, I'm a fucking dog, now I'm a monkey.

"Cuff him Donaldson. Let's see what this homeboy is hiding. *They* all got something to hide."

He cuffs me and pushes me down on the curb to sit like I'm on punishment. Cars are driving by slowly. Folks can't help but to be nosey when the police has someone pulled over. At this point, I'm scared shitless. I don't know if they are going to plant something on me, if they are going to rough me up or say that I resisted arrest and kill me. I still don't know why I got pulled over. I'll be damned if I ask now. I can't remember the last time that I prayed, but I sit there and pray that I make it home alive and promise God that I'll be a better man, father and boyfriend.

"Peter is that you?"

I never thought I'd be happy to hear her voice.

"Yes Ms. Miller, it's me."

When I look up, I see her with a white girl that I don't recognize. She is out of her uniform and in a tank top and spandex.

"What's going on? Why are you in cuffs?" Ms. Miller asks.

Just as she says that the two cops notice them standing there. The cop that scared me with his night stick says "Tell your hoes that their zaaaaaddy will be in jail tonight. So, they can take the night off." *This white boy watches too much TV.*

The other cop looks at the two women and tries to stop his partner from saying something stupid. He realizes that it is too late. He must be a rookie.

I was out of cuffs and back in my car after a one-minute conversation between the ladies and the cops. When the ladies were done the cops were both red and apologetic. I don't know what they said, but I later found out that the white girl my PO was jogging with is a county Police Commissioner. My PO told me to go to the RMV right now to get my registration renewed and to make sure that I'm in her office on time next Monday. She doesn't have to worry. I'll be on time. A nigger might even show up early.

4

PRODUCTS OF SEGREGATION

Jean:

My meeting was at the Hyatt in Baltimore. I booked my room for the night there too. The meeting went well. I had to wear my shirt that I had packed for tomorrow because I smelled like the Indian dude from the flight. I threw the shirt that I was wearing on the plane out. That's how contaminated it was. Tide wouldn't be able to get that funk out.

It's 7pm. I log onto Facebook to see what places in the area it recommends for soul food. Ida B's Table pops up. If it wasn't raining out, I could walk there. Instead I arrange for an Uber to pick me up. I look up the menu online so that I can have an idea of what I want to order when I get there. Five minutes later my Uber driver is here.

I'm picked up in a silver Nissan Maxima. My driver's name is Chris. The car smells like pine. He has a tree air freshener hanging in the front and there's one in the passenger side door pocket. I roll down my window a little knowing that the rain is going to wet me up. It's not that I don't like smell of pine. It's just that I've had enough with overpowering smells for the day. Too much of anything isn't good.

He lets me out in front of Ida B's Table. It is inside of a brick building with a black sign. The words "Ida B's" is written with white lettering. Underneath it is the word "Table" written with red lettering. As soon as I walk in I'm greeted by my people. All the staff are black. I feel at home. I walk around and admire all the pictures on the walls. They're not just pictures—they're art.

A profile of Nina Simone is drawn on the wall where the hostess stands.

"The way to right wrongs is to turn the light of truth upon them-Ida B. Wells." I read this out loud as I stare at the drawing on the wall of her placed beside the quote. When I sit down, I look at the menu and the same quote is on the menu. Let's hope the food tastes as good as the atmosphere is making me feel. A young brother comes over to my table and takes my drink order. While he's here I give him my meal order too. I'm glad I looked at the menu ahead of time. I order Ida B's Hot Chicken, Sweet Potatoes, and Mac and Cheese.

I must have got here right on time. The place starts filling up quickly and I'm at a table that can seat four. When I first arrived, The place was pretty empty so I had my choice of spots to sit. This dude looks at me like he knows me, then approaches me.

"Hi, I'm Randy," he excitedly greets.

"Hey Randy. Is there something that I can do for you?"

"I'm so glad that you asked! Me and two of my friends are dying to eat here. We were told it is an hour wait. I see that you are here by yourself. Do you mind if we join you?" He asks.

"Damn, that's rather forward of you…."

"I know. I figured it was worth a try. Plus, I didn't get the homophobe vibe from you."

"What? The homophobe vibe? This should be an interesting conversation. Tell your crew that they are welcome to join me for dinner," I say. He waves them over.

"This is George and this is Jerome," Randy introduces them. George is skinny and short, five foot five tops. Jerome is my height about six feet and skinny too. They both shake my hand and thank me. Randy continues with the introductions.

"This is… I never got your name. Where are my manners? Your name is?"

"My name is Jean. Nice to meet everyone," I say laughing. Randy towers over me. He's built like a basketball player, lean and muscular with the height to match.

"Hi Jeeeeeeeean!" They all sing in unison.

"I've already ordered my drink and meal. Let me call the waiter over to get the rest of your orders," I say while waving to the waiter. The waiter returns and takes the rest of the orders. George breaks the ice.

"So, Jean, you got any children?"

"Nope. The closest thing I have to having children is my nephew. What about y'all? Am I sitting with a table of dads?" I ask as I take a sip of water.

"More like a table of fags," George says laughing. I almost choke on my water.

"Isn't that offensive to gays?" I ask. Randy chimes in.

"Only if it's coming from the mouth of someone who isn't gay," he says giggling.

"Kinda like the word 'Nigger'." I say. "If you're a person of color that uses the word, it's ok to say it amongst us. It's an entirely different evil when it's said by somebody outside of us."

"Jean, you don't even want to get us started with that. We will be here all day. You see Jerome sitting there all quiet and shit. Consider that a warning and a blessing. He's one of the righteous people that don't use the word in any situation. He even calls it the N-word like he's from outside of our race or some shit," Randy says shaking his head.

"I got something I'd like to hear Jean's opinion on," Randy and Jerome look at each other.

"How do you feel about Blacks being in the military?" George asks.

"Hell motherfu…," Randy cuts him off.

"I'm asking Jean his opinion. We know how you feel?" George asks and cuts his eyes at Randy.

"I am a live and let live dude. If a brother wants to join the military for whatever benefits he feels he and/or family would get, so be it. It's his life. If you're asking me if I'd want my theoretical son to join, I'd have to agree with and finish Randy's statement. Hell motherfucking no!"

"Finally, somebody with some common sense," Randy says pleased with my response. Jerome speaks.

"Why do you feel that way Jean?" Jerome gives me his undivided attention.

"Black men have a history of being rejected by White America. Did you know that during the Civil War, black men were willing to risk their lives for the Union but the Union rejected them at first? They all look at me like they don't believe me. All three gave me a stank face.

"Think about it. They weren't going to give black men the ok to kill white men. They feared the black man. These same black men were willing to fight for this country before they were even considered citizens."

"Hoooooold up! This is getting heavy. I'm gonna need a stronger drink for this," Randy says motioning for the waiter.

Jerome chimes in. "Oh yeah, Jean sounds like he's about to drop some serious KRS-1 knowledge on us. I laugh at his reference.

"If we are truly honest with ourselves, we will admit that the Civil War wasn't even about ending slavery. Abolishing slavery was just a bi-product of it. In the South, slave labor drove the economy. In the North, industry drove the economy. They were fighting over state sovereignty versus federal authority. It was over state's rights and the limits of federal power in a union of states. Who made the decisions about slavery—local institutions or a central government—was the matter in question. We were afterthoughts. We weren't a part of the constitution. We were amendments to it. Amendments 13-15 were for us. The abolishment of slavery, equal protection under the law, and the right to vote.

So, you ask if I think Blacks should be in the Military. No. I know Frederick Douglass would beg to differ. This country doesn't respect us. It doesn't represent us and it doesn't protect us. Why should we fight to preserve what's broken? They got some 'amendments' to make before we should fight for this place. Fuck that shit. Real talk. Class dismissed."

"Well damn, I didn't know we were having lunch with a black history professor," Randy jokes.

"More like Malcom X," Jerome slips in.

"If I shut my eyes and if you said devil one time in your monologue I would have sworn I was speaking to the Honorable Elijah Mohammed himself," George laughs.

"Oh, you brothers got jokes huh?" I say laughing with them.

We shut that place down. The food was bomb. We inhaled it. I'm surprised I even know what it tasted like. We talked about everything under the sun. We exchange numbers and say that we will keep in touch. I admit to them that I don't have any homosexual friends in my circle.

"Well now you got three. See how God works. He saw your need and fulfilled it," Randy says in a preacher like voice.

"I wouldn't go that far," I say cracking up.

"Who are you kidding? Next we will have you at the gay clubs with us," Jerome jokes.

"That'll happen when y'all start eating pussy."

"EEEEEWE! I guess you won't be in any gay clubs with us," Randy says shaking his head.

"I guess not" I say laughing.

The laughs were nonstop at Ida B's. Randy, George and Jerome were the best part of my trip. They ask if I want to meet up for breakfast at the same place tomorrow. I decline. My flight back to Boston is at noon. I'm going to sleep late and then head to the airport. I tell them this and they all boo me in unison. I can't wait to tell my sister about this crew. Not tonight though, tonight I am going straight to bed. I arrange for an Uber driver to pick me up. It's here in no time. We say our goodbye's again and I head back to the hotel.

I text Silvie to let her know that I am in my hotel room and about to go to sleep. I tell her that I am just letting her know that the I didn't succumb to the streets of Baltimore.

I'll catch up with her tomorrow. She doesn't text me back to say goodnight. I fall asleep.

Elijah:

I can't lie. It felt good to have Silvie show me some attention. And she's bold too. She kissed me with her hand strategically placed on the zipper of my pants just to see what I was working with. I can't believe she thought I was going to have hard ashy lips. Her lips were so soft. I could've kissed her all night.

I'm on the treadmill, at Planet Fitness, replaying what took place in Silvie's car as if it was my favorite scene in a movie. I look down and I've already jogged for twenty minutes. I need to daydream more often; it made the time fly by. I have ten more minutes until I move on to the machines. I tend to do a lot of my planning while I am jogging on the treadmill. I plan my night and my tomorrow. I live one day at a time. That's the only way that I can mentally handle this type of living. Don't get me wrong, I think about my long-term future. I do have a game plan. I am not trying to be out here after the New Year. Tomorrow's a big day for me.

The sweat dripping from my head is making it hard for my earphones to stay in. The left one keeps popping out. I'm getting irritated because I have to keep adjusting them.

Last year, this time, I would have just thrown these out and went and bought a pair of better headphones. No biggie. This year making a move like that is a luxury. I'm in no position to spend money on new head phones. Being poor makes life so inconvenient. Langston Hughes said it best "It is such a bore being always poor."

I change my music to listen to something that is going to get me through these last ten minutes on the treadmill. I put on Kendrick Lamar's song "I". I start rapping with my hands like I'm in a rap video. I know that I must be loud because folks keep looking at me. I'm in my zone and can't be bothered with their looks of disapproval. These lyrics speak to me. These folks should focus on listening to what I'm saying instead of focusing on the fact that I'm loud. I rap the entire song while jogging on the treadmill.

I'm hyped now. Here comes the hook. If they thought I was loud before, they're going to think I'm screaming now. I don't give a fuck. They need to hear this. They need to hear me. I don't have a home to go to after my work out, they do. That shit's only temporary though. In the words of that motivational speaker from Baltimore-Van Brooks, "Ain't nobody gonna outwork me."

As I sing the hook, this elderly white man gives me a dirty look as he walks by. He's walking towards the front desk. The staff is on the phone. He stands there with a pissed look on his face. The staff at the desk mouth's "one moment" to the perturbed white man. Next verse.

Here comes the hook. I look up and I see the elderly white man complaining to the staff and pointing at me. Normally, I try to keep a low key. I don't want any problems. Today, I'm on some "fuck you" shit. The hook is done. I look down at the tread mill to check my time. I have five minutes left. I look back at the staff desk. The white man walks away looking at me as he wipes the sweat off his red face. I meet his glare. He can't whoop me. I don't know who he thinks he's scaring but it's not me. From the corner of my eyes I see the staff walking towards me.

I shut my eyes as if I'm really into my music and my work out. I then sing the last verse of Kendrick's song. I open my eyes because I hear the same lyrics I'm rapping being said by someone else. He's young with a black Mohawk that has purple dye at the tips. His purple Planet Fitness shirt says STAFF on the back. I guess I shouldn't have been surprised that he's a Kendrick Lamar fan. I bet the elderly white man didn't expect this. In unison, the young man with the Mohawk stands in front of my treadmill and finishes the verse with me. If the old guy thought I was loud before, this is really going to disturb him. The two of us rap like we are both Kendrick.

Mohawk gives me dap and then leaves. He walks back to the desk smiling. I can't say I would have imagined that exchange. The black dude at the desk is cracking up. The elderly white guy gets off the elliptical machine heated, and not from his work out. He storms off to the men's room. I get off the treadmill and decide to do free weights instead. It's funny how life is. It was looking like rap music was causing a clear divide between me and the white man. Instead it brought a black man and a white man together. The staff looked no older than twenty-one. The elderly white man should have joined us. It would have been a Kumbaya moment.

A black dude in a Black Genetically Resilient hoodie comes over to me as I sit down to do my arm curls. *I need that hoodie in my life.*

"Yo! I saw what went down. That shit was funny as hell. I knew that old white guy was gonna complain. He kept grilling you. I guess he thought that his stares would get you to stop. He learned today though. We got a few allies out there in Caucasia. That white boy was doing his thang." He says laughing. "By the way, my name is Shawn and you are?"

"Elijah, and nice to meet you Shawn. Your sweat shirt is dope."

"Ain't it? I got this at the Black Market in Dudley. There's this author that sells them. You should check the place out."

Dude talked more than he worked out. Normally, I don't like it when folks talk to me while working out, but he seemed like he needed someone to talk to. I felt like a female while I exchanged numbers with him. When he asked me where I live, I told him that it's complicated. He accepted that. We moved on. By the end of our conversation, he asked if I happened to have any Aleve. I still have five Ibuprofen left. I told him that I didn't have any—I didn't offer any Ibuprofen either. I gave him my ear. That's enough giving for today.

Shawn:

I heard this black dude singing that Kendrick Lamar song "I". I knew that it would be only a matter of time before one of the white people complained. He was loud, but you could tell he was in the zone. He was really feeling the lyrics. Well, it didn't go down the way that I thought it would. I mean, as expected, a white person did complain to the Planet Fitness staff, but the staff ended up shocking the hell out of me. Instead of asking the man on the treadmill to lower his voice, he went over there and started rapping with him. This was a white boy doing this shit. It was mad funny. It wasn't even the hook that he was singing. He knew the verse better than I did, and I'm black!

He came over to where I was using the free weights. I started up a conversation with him and we did more talking than we did reps. Actually, I did most of the talking. I just met him and I was telling him my life story. Well, not my life story, just my most recent significant event. What I realized is that I needed to talk about it. I hadn't talked to anyone about it. The person that I would have vented to is the person that caused me all this pain. I know that I caught him off guard when I asked him for his number. His facial expression spoke for him. I think he felt sorry for me. He gave me his number but based off his reaction, Elijah is probably hoping that I don't call him. I didn't want to scare him off so, I told him that I just started getting serious about my health and would love to work out with him. Nothing more. That's partially the truth. Me needing a new friend is the truth I omitted.

As I'm driving home, I think about my next move. I still can't figure out where and when Nakia and Peter snuck off to fuck. I try to think of long periods of time that Nakia and I weren't together. Then it dawns on me. When she went to get her hair done must have been it. *Damn.* I was stupid. She had me thinking that she was up in the hair salon for six hours. She must have been with him. That's not to say that she didn't get her hair done. She was deceitful enough to actually go to the salon.

I didn't pick up on it when she switched her routine up. In the past, Nakia came back home with her hair looking like she was going to a black-tie event. The first time she came home with her hair wrapped in this stretchy white paper, I should have been more suspicious. She's slick. She set the stage so that I wouldn't know if she got it done or not. Bitch.

I get mad all over again. I decide that I'm going to do one more thing to let Nakia know that it is not ok to stomp somebody's heart out of their chest. It is not ok to lie, cheat, and ruin a twenty-year friendship. If she thinks she can just walk away free from punishment, she is crazy. She is going to feel like she is having an asthma attack and can't catch her breath, no matter how hard she tries. There will be no inhaler to aid her. There was nobody there to help me catch my breath. She took my heart and my best-friend. Fuck her.

I am home now. It's cold in here, but not as cold as Nakia. I'm pissed because I forgot to set the timer for the heat. *You forgot to guard you heart too,* I hear my mind say. I walk over to the wall where my picture of Nefertiti hangs. The thermostat shares the same wall. I turn the heat on seventy-five degrees. Normally, I wouldn't turn it up so high, but I'm freezing.

It is so cold that I can't even move around the house comfortably. I locate my space heater, turn it on and sit down on my recliner with my gray fleece blanket. I haven't sat in this chair since…

The blanket smells like her. It's too cold to take the blanket off, but I'm repulsed by it. I want to go take a shower. Instead, I sit still. I try to sink into the leather of my dark brown reclining chair. I'm too tense. I'm experiencing a combination between my body having a physiological response to my emotional state and the cold. My clothes are still wet from working out. That's not helping. The blanket isn't helping either. I start to shiver. My teeth start to chatter involuntarily. I can't generate any heat and the space heater is pointed directly at me. I get mad at myself again for forgetting to set my timer for the heat.

I'm mad at myself for loving someone that would suck the dick of my best friend. I am mad at myself for believing that a woman could be a virgin at her age. Most girls aren't virgins past tenth grade these days. I should have known better. This girl had me masturbating to the idea of being inside of her virgin pussy. I was willing to wait only because nobody else had ever had it. Had it been someone that just decided that they wanted to be celibate until marriage I wouldn't have been with the shit. This was a special circumstance. This bitch goes and gives it away to my best friend. I feel tears swell up in my eye but I fight them. I haven't cried yet and I'm not about to start now. I'm too fucking mad to cry.

I haven't decided how I am going to get back at Peter yet. Best believe he will get his too. I know that he can be a piece of shit when he wants to, but we've never went through any type of betrayal like this. This shit right here is unforgiveable. People get killed for shit like this. I take that back. People get killed for less than this. I've had this nigga's back since high school. Kids at school used to tell me that he would talk shit about me behind my back. I just let it ride because I know that he was upset about his home life. Back then, he had anger problems and I felt bad for him. I understood though, he had good reasons to be mad. He just had a habit of misdirecting his anger.

I put up with his funky moods, fuck-ups and temper tantrums for two decades and this is what I get in return. He fucks me over by fucking the woman that I was going to marry. I wouldn't believe it if I didn't hear with my own ears. Even when I did hear it with my own ears, I didn't believe it. I had to have a conversation with myself for it to sink in. I've been having more and more of those conversations with myself these days.

I really thought that I found my true love; the woman that I was going to grow old with. I had already started daydreaming about what our kids would look like and how they'd behave. I thought about getting a house for us to start our life in as a married couple. I was planning for our future. I even set her up as my beneficiary on my life insurance policies. I need to make sure that I change that. I'll be damned if she gets a dime off me for anything. She's taken enough. I've surrounded myself with a bunch of takers. It's my turn to start taking shit.

Jean:

I call Silvie to check in on her. The last time that I texted her, I was in Baltimore. She didn't respond until the next day. When she did, it was short. All she wrote back was *ok*. That's not like her. She's that person that likes to text paragraphs. Here we are a week later and I still haven't heard a peep from her. It's my day to pick up my nephew. I call her to confirm to see if I am picking him up or if she is dropping him off.

"Hello," she answers.

"Where you been? I texted you my last night in Baltimore to let you know that I was good and didn't hear from you until the next day. Not only did I not hear from you until the next day, but your short response was out of character for you."

"I'm sorry big brother, I was busy." Silvie says as if it was rehearsed.

"Busy? Busy doing what?" I ask wondering what's up with my sister.

"I've just been busy. You know running around doing this and that. I'm sorry Jean. I figured you had enough women keeping you busy that you wouldn't even take notice. What's up with you? All of your women mad at you this week?"

"You think you can flip it without me noticing. I'm the King of recognizing bullshit. Of all the sisters I deal with, don't be careless and think that you can pull one over on me too. I was raised by a black woman and I date nothing but black women. I know y'all very well. So, what is it that you aren't telling me?" She starts laughing. I knew she was hiding something.

"Well…" she drags out.

"Well what?" I say impatiently.

"I've kinda been seeing someone new."

Here we go with some bullshit. I know my sister. She has horrible taste in men. She likes them tall, dark and handsome. She usually ends up with men that are tall, dark and looking for handouts. My nephew's father is by far the worst and she had a baby with him. I'm happy that she didn't marry him. At one point her gullible behind was talking about it. Thank God he cheated before she ran with that idea. I take that back. Thank God that she found out that he was cheating before she followed through with the idea of getting married to the bum. We know that he was cheating way before she found out. That's why my nephew has a sister that is the same age as him.

"What's his name? Where'd you meet him? How many kids by different women does he have?"

"Damn Jean. Why do you have to be so negative?" She whines.

"Just answer the question."

"I met him at the shelter. His name is Elijah and he doesn't have any kids," she says as if she's proud and expects me to be proud too.

"Hmm, that sounds suspicious. Are you dating a teenager? All black men our age have kids by now."

"You don't," she shoots back.

"I'm the exception. I'm also a unicorn. Are you telling me that you found another unicorn?"

"Geesh Jean. Your cynicism makes it hard to talk to you about my relationships," Silvie complains.

"Oh wait! You said that you're 'kinda' seeing someone. Now you're using the word relationship. Who is this dude? Where does he work? Please don't tell me he's light skin."

There's silence. I repeat my question.

"Where does he work Silvie? Please tell me this nigga ain't working at the mall at one of those kiosks," I say half-jokingly. It's apparent that she doesn't appreciate my humor. She's on the defense.

"It's none of your business where he works Jean!" She says a little too loud and strong for my liking.

"Why is that such a hard question to answer. There must be some truth to what I've said or else you'd have told me where he works. Instead you're getting defensive."

"Listen to how you come at me Jean! You talk to me as if you're my dad and not my brother."

"You and I know that can't possibly be the case. We've never met our dad. So, that's not a good comparison. Now if you're talking about how a dad is supposed to look out for a daughter, then maybe so. I feel like I'm just being a loving brother. It's funny that you have a problem with me acting like your 'dad' now, but you've never had a problem with it whenever you've accepted money from me," I spit back at her.

"You really just said that? You felt that was necessary? It's like that between us now where we take shit below the belt to get our points across? That's really messed up Jean." She sounds hurt, but I don't back down.

"Silvie you better go ahead with all of that. It sounds like you caught some of that victim mentality that your son's father is diseased with. Ain't nothing changed with me. I call it how I see it. You got a history of dealing with weak-ass niggas. I'm trying to find out if history is repeating itself. After a while, you have to take a look at yourself to see if you bring this shit on yourself. Don't get me wrong, these dudes you've dealt with did you wrong, but some of that is your fault."

"Oh word? Why don't you tell me how you really feel?" Silvie spits. I know she's heated, but she needs to hear this.

"Your head gets a little big because you think a good-looking man picked you over some other chick. You feel good because these niggas are showing you a little bit of attention. They tell you how fine you are and how good of a person you are. And you eat that shit right up. Then they test you."

"How the hell do you know?" Silvie says with an attitude.

"I know all types of dudes, Silvie. The type you keep picking are opportunist. I know how they operate or should I say run game. You're an easy target. I know you because I am your brother. If they wait long enough or listen hard enough, they'll know how to hook you. You're a giver. They'll figure that out if they pay attention to your routine. You go to church every Sunday and think it's important to tithe. You go to the shelter on weekends to volunteer. You don't have you son's father signed up for child support through the court system. You'll go half on a meal with a grown ass man. You're a fair person. You show that by giving people the benefit of the doubt all the time. You're an opportunist's dream."

"And you're a woman's worst nightmare," she says defensively. I ignore her.

"Here's how it goes. They make you think that you love them. Next, they set you up for the kill—whatever that may be. Maybe they charge up your credit cards, by having you charge shit for them. Maybe, they give you a sob story about their finances because they saw the word sucker tattooed on your ass when you let them hit it after the first night. These niggas give you an orgasm and then ask you to co-sign on a car for them. The bums you deal with don't stop there. They're the type to take you to the car dealership and make you think that you're co-signing. When you get there, he finds out that his credit is so bad that he can't get a car even with you as a co-signer. Best believe he knew his credit was fucked up before you got there. So, he goes for the kill and asks you to buy it. He promises to make the payments. You love him, so you do it. It's always down-hill from there."

"You sound like you are speaking from experience Jean." She's beyond pissed.

"Silvie, you always get burnt in the end. You heart gets broken. You end up with bad credit and I know you've had to have had an STD a few times. You don't even have to tell me. I already know. So, yes, I may be a little harsh with you and your relationships. You're shitty when it comes to judging character. I'm tired of hearing about how this one did this and how the last one did that."

"Oh, you don't have to worry about hearing anything else from me-believe that," Silvie says.

"When the fuck are you going to get it right? Leave these sorry ass dudes alone. They don't love you. They just want pussy and whatever else you can give. Shit. You ain't got much. That should tell you a lot about them. I'd feel better if you were out here like the sisters I seem to always run into. They make sure a brother has money to put inside their pocketbook before they give them any pussy. They definitely ain't giving dudes any of their money. I'd respect you more." I say with finality.

"Well I guess you got everything off your chest. You sure told me about myself Jean. Do you feel good? I had no idea that I was such a poor excuse for a black woman.

My own brother doesn't even have compassion for me. I now understand how you could talk to me in such a disgusting way. You said it. You don't respect me. That hurt.

"I'm sorry Silvie, bu-" She cuts me off.

"You know what else hurts me. It hurts that you can't allow me to be happy. Who knows what this could be? It could be another failed relationship, another poor judgment of character. He could end up being everything that you've said I've had before. Even so, that doesn't give you the right to snatch my small moment of happiness and you know exactly what I'm talking about. The happiness that comes with being in a new relationship. The happiness that comes with being excited about seeing each other. The happiness that comes with doing something nice for the other just because. Oh wait... you don't know anything about that. Of course not."

"How could you think that I wouldn't know anything about that. You're sounding real emotional right now Silvie."

"I'm gonna need you to shut up and let me finish my thought. Dear brother, you are in and out of pussy so much that the newness has worn off. You're numb. You call yourself looking for your black queen but all you seem to be doing is sampling the queendom. It's sad that you don't assess your own behavior but you did a real good job assessing mine. Don't you know that you won't ever find your queen until you let yourself be ok with a woman being flawed. You have to be ok with a woman not having it all together. What the hell would she need you for if she had everything she needed at the table. And it's ok not to have it all together. People get in relationships to weather storms life brings as a stronger force together and to share the joys that life brings with someone that sees past their flaws and finds beauty. They want to be with someone that lifts them up. It's not all about the pockets. Don't get me wrong, building wealth is great, but building an impenetrable bond with someone that loves you is greater."

"Is that what you've experienced Silvie—impenetrable bonds?" I ask sarcastically.

"You know what big brother, I feel bad for you. I feel bad that you're looking for a queen that you just want to build wealth instead of building sustainability. You'll never find love looking for someone that has it all together. There's nothing to build if they've already built it. Ask yourself what you bring to the table. Maybe you're not the unicorn you claim to be. Maybe you're just like these brothers out here you are warning me of. You may not take money from women the way that other men do, but you, like them, are an opportunist. You want a woman that has it all together so that you don't have to work. Just like them, you don't want to work for it. With that being said, I'll end this conversation by saying I'm going to take your advice and stop dealing with 'opportunists'. And guess what, I'm starting with you. Oh, and one more thing… FUCK YOU NIGGA!" She screams and hangs up the call.

5

MAMMY WHO?

Elijah:

I been on a high since I went on my job interview a few days ago. I don't know if I'll get it, but I think I definitely earned a second interview. I was told that they'll call candidates on Friday if they are interested in conducting a second interview. I interviewed for a case management position at a biotech company. I have the experience. I worked at another company doing the same type of work, but they had to let a handful of people go when they didn't get FDA approval for this medication that would slow the progression of renal failure. I only worked there a year and a half. I left with a severance check and a promise of another job from a former co-worker. He left a few months before the lay-off to work for another company.

Things changed quickly in a month's time. The co-worker that promised me a position at the place he was working at couldn't make good on the promise. I broke up with my girlfriend. I lost my housing and became homeless with just a severance check to live on. I never saw myself being homeless. I don't have a drug addiction. I am not an alcoholic. I don't have any mental health issues. I don't have a criminal background. I'm not lacking in education. I have a master's degree. My mistake is that I lived from paycheck-to-paycheck.

I didn't plan ahead. I didn't put money aside. I didn't plan for a rainy day. I lived like things would always stay the same. I knew better. My grandmother hipped me to channel 126 Urban View on Sirius satellite radio. The Karen Hunter Show equipped me with the tools I needed to stay ahead of the game. I just didn't use them. They sat in the toolbox collecting dust instead of collecting money. I never thought it would happen to me. I'm sure that nobody thinks that it will ever happen to them. The truth is, a small shift in the weather can create the perfect storm. There are a lot of us who are just a few shifts in the weather away from homelessness.

My purpose is greater than my current circumstance. I've been blessed to have a grandmother that made sure I knew who God was, what he can do and what he's done for me. That is the best gift and guidance anyone has ever given me. I get my self-esteem, my resilience and my common-sense from her. There is no doubt about that. I usually check in on her at the nursing home before I go to the shelter on Saturdays. I hope that I will be able to tell her that I have a new job. I haven't told her that I am homeless, but she's not stupid. She doesn't miss much. She knows something is up. Today is her birthday so I'm seeing her today instead of my usual Saturday visit.

The 450 bus lets me off on the corner of Western Ave and Chatham Street in Lynn. The weather is changing. It's getting colder. The cold wind makes my eyes water as I step off the bus. Cold days mean even colder nights. I need to be off these streets before the first snow storm. I go inside of the Western Ave. corner store. An Indian dude greets me and I ask him if I can use an Amex gift card in his store. He tells me that I can, just not for the lottery. Good thing I have scratch tickets already. My grandmother only asks for scratch tickets on her birthday. I grab some of her favorite snacks: a box of honey buns, a box of oatmeal cream pies and a mini apple pie. I walk over to the freezer where I see most of the ice cream looks frost bitten. I grab a French vanilla single serving of ice-cream to go with her apple pie. Everything comes to twenty-five dollars. I make a mental note to remember the balance left on the card.

I exit the store and again my eyes water. It feels like it got colder while I was in the store. I was only in there for five minutes. I'm probably just cold from handling the ice-cream. The cheap knit gloves that I have on have a few holes in them. I need to use the other twenty-five dollars left on the Amex gift card and buy some warmer gloves. As I walk down Chatham street, I notice an older Asian man going through green trash bins with blue covers. It's trash day.

He looks like he's had a productive day. He has at least three trash bags full of cans in a Market Basket carriage. He has on a what looks like and old-school Triple Fat Goose full length coat. His boots look like Timberland work boots, but the closer I get to him; I can see that they are not. He has on corduroys that are doo-doo brown. The coat takes up most of the length of his body. Only a small section of his legs can be seen. I look at his hands as he lifts the blue cover to the what I now see is a recycling bin. He has on the gloves that I need. I recognize the tag. They are winter thinsulate black gloves. I'm going to walk to

Walmart after I finish visiting my grandmother. I should be able to pick up some warm gloves for a decent price there.

Unless I cross the street, I have to pass him on the sidewalk to get to the nursing home. I expect him to tense up a little, as most do when they are alone and see a big black man coming their way. He surprises me and looks me in my eyes and speaks.

"Good day today, yes?" The Asian man says. His face looks weather beaten. What he has on his head is what immediately gets my attention.

"I can't complain," I answer. He continues.

"Complaining will get you nowhere very fast," he says laughing. I laugh with him. He notices me staring at his hat. And looks at me as if he wants to say "What's up? You good?"

I break the silence and the stare. "Oh, I'm sorry for staring. I was just noticing your hat."

"You like, yes? Someone drop it. You know Vision Space? Downtown Lynn. It has colorful picture outside and nice pictures inside. There I found it. It's nice, yes? Nice saying. I wear it when I collect bottles."

"Looks like you had a good day," I say sincerely.

"Yes! Yes, good day. I do this on my days off every week. Make good money. Able to help grandson with school books," he says proudly.

"Is your grandson in college?" I ask.

"UMass. He study business. He very smart. Proud of him. I come out here to help family. Family is everything, yes?" He says smiling. I agree with him.

"Yes. Family is everything," I say goodbye and keep it moving. I think about how the hat couldn't have been found by a more appropriate person. He is definitely "Genetically Resilient." He's out here in these streets to help his grandson pay for books for school. That's twice this week I've seen someone with apparel that has "Genetically Resilient" written across it. When I get my apparel, I'm going to get two pieces. I know my grandmother would love one. Christmas will be here before you know it. I'll get us both something for Christmas. Hopefully, I'll be receiving a paycheck from my job by then. I put my headphones on and zone out to Kendrick Lamar's album *Damn*. I have a ten-minute walk to the nursing home.

***

I push the handicap button with my elbow so that the nursing home entrance doors open hands-free. They open, but they are slow as hell. It's as if the doors are in slow motion because most of the people on the other side of the doors are too. I laugh to myself. The nursing home has elderly doors.

I smile as I walk to the front desk that's situated over to right side of the building. I greet the older white woman at the desk. She's super friendly. She told me her name the first time I visited my grandmother here but I forget her name. She doesn't have a name tag on. I just say hello, ask her how she's doing and sign my name in the visitor's book. I walk to the elevator. My grandmother is only on the second floor. Theoretically, I could take the stairs, but they use some type of a code to get in and out of the staircase. It's too much trouble to do all of that so I take the elevator up one flight.

When the doors to the elevator open, the nurses' station is the first thing I see. I greet the small crew of Haitian and African nurse and head to my grandmother's room. It smells like too much Fabuloso floor cleaner with an aftertaste of urine. I scrunch my face up as I walk down the corridor. My grandmother's room is at the end of the hall.

Originally, her room was at the beginning of the hall. She said that she wanted to be moved because too many people were passing her room and making too much noise. She felt that if she was placed at the end of the hall, the only people that would be walking by would be folks that were coming down there to see her or her roommate.

She was right. The foot traffic is far less at her end of the hall. I pull out my phone anticipating her smile. I want to record it. I enter the room and an older black gentleman dressed as if he's going to church, is sitting on the chair that I usually sit in when I visit. He sees me and stands up. My grandmother looks at me and waves her hand as if she's dismissing me. She directs her attention back to the man that was sitting in my seat.

"Where you going Rufus? That's just my grandson Lijah. You don't have to go. He can pull up another chair."

He tells her that maybe he'll see her later in the evening. I'm wondering what the fuck that means. Why does it have to be in the evening? Why didn't he say later in the day? Let me find out that my grandmother has a boo up inside this nursing home. That better be all he is up inside. I quickly try to erase the thought of my grandmother getting some from Rufus.

I put my phone away. That smile I expected was replaced with a dismissive wave.

"Whatchu doing here Lijah? It ain't Saturday."

"Nana, you really think that I'd miss your birthday? You know me better than that," I say.

"You're right. I do know you. So, come clean. What haven't you been telling me?" She says as if she has a sixth sense. I'm convinced that she does.

I come right out and tell her. She's a no-nonsense type of woman. She doesn't want to hear the fluff. She wants the raw uncut version and I give it to her. I tell her how life has changed for me since the summer. She listens with a straight face. She's deliberate with her lack of emotion. She's hard to read and she prefers it that way. I haven't mastered that gift incredible skill yet. My facial expressions are louder than anything I could ever say out of my mouth.

As I am saying everything out loud, I feel myself getting overwhelmed. My grandmother extends her arms to me. I hug her and I let the tears fall. There is no sound with these tears. It's more of a release than a sob. It is a brief moment where I have permission to be vulnerable. I have permission to let my guard down. My grandmother holds me for a good two-minutes. There's nothing like a grandmother's hug. There's also nothing like their wisdom.

"You straight?" My grandmother says as more of a statement than a question.

"I'm good Nana. Thank you," I say with the hope of sounding confident. She goes on.

"Let me tell you something Lijah. You ain't the first black man to struggle. You won't be the last either. It's hard out here for a black man in these streets. It's even harder not to fall victim to them. I know that there aren't many incentives to take the right road when the road you're on is hard enough; but, you gotta do your best to stay strong and focus on the end game," she advises.

"I know Nana. You taught me better than that. I haven't forgotten about the end game. That's why I don't pay the dope dealers any mind when they call me crazy for choosing to live on the street, instead of doing a few jobs for them until I get back on my feet. Trust me Nana. I know the math. The risks outweigh the rewards," I say reassuring her that I'm not out here in these streets acting crazy.

"Yes. We don't need you adding to the stereotype Lijah. If you let the Honkies tell it, they'd swear that the black man is the reason why there is so much crime. Y'all are stereotyped as violent, aggressive men prone to crime. The black man has held that stereotype as long as I been living. The truth is the stereotype was created to divert the attention away from the real problem at hand. And then they solidified it by creating a system to damn near guarantee an unfavorable outcome for black men."

I look at her because she used the word divert and solidified in her sentence. She smiles at me.

"Yeah, I said divert. You think you the only person in this family with a vocabulary. Just because I don't use big words doesn't mean that I don't know big words. Lijah, don't start acting like them. You know, we started off in this country with no opportunities. We were slaves. Ever since we got our freedom, they have been trying to take it back. They've settled for crippling us-by limiting our resources and opportunities to be successful in this country. Stereotyping has been an effective tactic in keeping the black man down. There's another big word for you, college boy. No opportunity means no path to success."

I try to make myself comfortable on the hard visitor's chair that's positioned beside her bed. I know this is going to be one of Nana's talks that feel like sermons.

"Since they've blocked our paths, we've had to dig tunnels to survive. Here's some math and vocabulary for you. These paths that I'm talking about—the ones that the honkies been blocking—they equate to the black man having limited and inadequate opportunities. I see the news. I listen to the Karen Hunter Show. There's a reason why some black men are out here doing home invasions and robbing folks. They're hungry and it don't have to be for food. If you ain't never been hungry, you won't understand. But let's use food as a simple example.

"Ok. I'm with you...food," I say letting her know that I'm paying attention.

"Imagine that you haven't eaten for days. You got no money and no opportunity to make any. What do you do? I'll tell you what you do. You do what you gotta do to survive. Uh oh...I feel a big word coming on Lijah. Wait for it... it's called self-preservation. Do you think that if there were an abundance of job opportunities for Black men there'd be as much crime? Most crime is done out of desperation. Black people find ways to make a way. When those ways lead to an arrest, they get their scarlet letter, which is their criminal record. That scarlet letter sets them up for having even fewer opportunities than they did before the criminal record. Remember what I mentioned earlier about the systems honkies put in place. Well, there goes a taste of one."

"Honkies Nana?" I interrupt. She sucks her teeth in return.

"Now, these black men have a choice to make. They can take the long, straight and very narrow road which offers no promises? On that same road is a job that doesn't pay enough to support a family. Or they can go the crooked road and step their game up in that street life to give their family a fighting chance? Either way, they are a victim to the stereotype inflicted upon them. Shit ain't easy for a black man," She ends.

"Damn Nana. You sound like you're a black man!" I say laughing, but very impressed with her insight.

"I know you have an opinion about the state of the black man Lijah. If you don't, you should. You should always know where you stand. Tell your grandmother where you stand." She looks at me knowingly. She knows I can be passionate and longwinded when I feel strongly about an issue.

I'm about to remind her who her Lijah is. I stand up from the uncomfortable chair and walk to the foot of her bed. She's about to get a Law and Order closing statement. She's the judge and the jury. I clear my throat and straighten the tie that I'm not wearing. She has a huge grin on her face. She's ready to be entertained. Then she becomes a stoic judge and gives me the nod to proceed.

"Yes. The black man is stereotyped and his life is at risk every day because of it. He has to think about how he's being perceived every moment. Do you know how stressful that is? The stereotype follows him wherever he goes. The stereotype follows him to work in the morning. It follows him driving to church on Sunday. It follows him on the train on his way to a Celtics game. It follows him to the North End to get some Italian food. It follows him to Suffolk University on his way to his classes. It follows him to his white girlfriend's apartment in Saugus. Then with his hands up and his back against the wall, the stereotype corners him."

I throw my hands up for effect. "The threat of attack is always present. White people use the police like a whip of a slave owner. It could hurt you or kill you. Either way the whip always leaves a scar. The psychological scar is far worse than the physical scar.

What perpetuates the stereotype? Fear does. It's instinctual for Whites to be fearful? They fear us because they've been inhumane to us. They stole us, made of slaves, broke our families a part and made it illegal for us to be in a position of power. Their fear stems from their subconscious admittance that they deserve punishment.

Until they are ready to take their ass whooping and relinquish their wealth and power, they will continue with business as usual."

I walk back over to the chair beside Nana's bed. Nana gathers her make believe notes and announces that court will recess until tomorrow morning. She bangs her imaginary gavel and smiles. She smiles so hard it looks like her dentures are going to pop out.

"That's right Lijah. Knowing how them honkies move will make it easier for you to narrate your life. How you think I've lived this long? I've been playing chess with them my entire life. I let them think that I only knew how to play checkers," she says howling with laughter.

"Nana I love spending time with you. You always lift my spirits and give me something to think about. On an even more serious note, with all that is stacked against me, it's real easy to feel hopeless. But know this, I am your grandson. I may be homeless, but hopeless I will never be." I lean over and give her a kiss on the cheek for added reassurance.

"Enough with all this heavy talk. This is supposed to be a birthday visit! Can we celebrate now?"

Nana raises her eyebrows and says "That all depends on if you got any goodies and scratch tickets in that bag of yours." We both laugh.

Shawn:

Be careful of what you tell your special somebody. Things change. One day they may no longer hold that title. I am only able to do what I am about to do today, because of what my former special somebody told me. Today's disclosure will crumble a few foundations. I have my favorite cousin to thank for this. She called to check-in on me. She's someone I've always been able to keep it real with. I told her that I was still hurting. I haven't healed totally because I am still bitter.

She suggested that I needed to figure out what I have to do to get it out of my system. "Do it, then move on," she said. I value her advice. I know that she's speaking from experience. She's had a tough life full of drama—movie worthy drama.

Her mom had a tragic life and death. Her dad lived a double life and was murdered. She has an addiction to sex. It has her doing all types of scandalous shit. I couldn't even begin to get into it. Shit is wild man. Yet, with everything she's been through, I trust her the most.

I am going to take her advice. I am going to let this shit go and move on, but not before one last attack of the heart. I tell her everything that she needs to know to execute. She has a connect at Channel Five News.

"So, you are one hundred percent positive that this has occurred. I can't be spreading fake news. I'll lose my credibility." She asks and states at the same time.

"Yes. Nakia told me this when she was mad at her sister for acting high and mighty because she is a pastor's wife. They got into an argument. I remember Nakia telling her sister that she's acting like she's never sinned. She told her to stop judging people so damn much," I tell my cousin.

"Ok good. I just need to do a little digging to make sure that I can corroborate what you are telling me. Once I can, this shit will be all over the news by the weekend. Now, you're sure that this is the route that you want to take? I haven't made any calls yet. You can still turn back and decide to just move on," she says.

"Cuz, I'm sure." I say with finality. I can hear her smiling through the phone.

"We are definitely family. That settles it. Leave it to Karma." she says laughing at her play with words. Nakia and everyone she loves will feel this.

On the other hand, Peter is a creature of habit. It will be easy to set him up for failure. There are two things that he consistently struggles with, being monogamous and keeping a roof over his head. This guy changes his address with every new relationship. He never has a place of his own. He lives with whatever woman he's with at the time. There's one thing that I can count on that will help me with what I have planned for him. Whatever woman he is with now, he's cheating on her. He can't keep his dick in his pants. He always wants something different. It doesn't matter if he's happy with his woman at the time. It doesn't matter if the new woman has a man. And worst of all, it doesn't matter if it's your best-friend's fiancée.

I've never hated anyone, until now. Nobody has ever tried to murder me emotionally the way that Peter has. That nigga *I hate*. I hate him, but to accomplish what I have in store for him, I'm going to have to show him love. I'm going to have to pick back up where we left off like I don't know that he played me. As a matter of fact, I'm going to call him right now.

The voice message comes on. I leave a message.

"Hey! What's good? Just seeing what you trying to get into. Hit me back."

I've just set the stage. Now, I'll wait on him. As soon as I leave the message, my phone rings.

I answer. "Hello."

"What's good!" Peter shouts.

"I'm trying to see what's good with you. Whatchu getting into?" I ask but could care less.

"I'm glad you called. You trying to run these streets with me tonight?

"Yeah. What time you trying to go out? What spot are we hitting first?"

We talk for a few more minutes and then hang up. I'm going to have to tap into my inner Denzel Washington to pull this shit off. I despise this fool. It's on the level where I wouldn't even attend his funeral. He's dead to me. But for the purposes of emotionally kicking this dude in his teeth, I will act like he's my brother. We will pick back up where we left off.

I have some time to kill before tonight so I turn on the TV to watch some of these reality shows. I'll need something to talk about with him. That way I can focus on something other than him fucking my fiancée. I decide to catch up on *Love and Hip Hop*. Peter will be sure to ask if I saw the latest episode and break it down as if he's a professional film critic.

Half-way through the episode, I feel a migraine coming on. I know that it is a migraine because the light is starting to bother me. I turn off the light and I feel a little relief. Nausea starts to creep in soon after. The roof of my mouth and the teeth surrounding it start to bother me. It's as if each one of my teeth decided to ache at the same time. My headache goes from a nagging throb to a full-blown thump. It's like the young Hispanic dude that just got his system in his car hooked up is driving around in my head blasting loud reggae ton music that rattles windows and sets off car alarms. I turn down the TV volume because I'm sensitive to sound. My headache is officially a migraine. This is not what I need tonight. How am I supposed to go to a club with a migraine? I lay down and hope that a pill will put these symptoms to rest.

Jean:

I'm back in Maryland for a about a week. I called Randy last night and made plans to hook up with the rest of the crew later at Ida B's for dinner. This time I'm out here for a conference. I'll be here for four days, but I decided that I'm going to extend my trip into the weekend and see what Maryland is all about. It gets a bad rap for the high crime rate. That's what the media reports, but I know that there is more to the city than that. They aren't going to make me afraid of my own people.

Keynote speaker Van Brooks told a story that damn near brought me to tears of joy and pain. Real talk, if I was at home watching him I would have cried. This brother told a story of inspiration, determination and victory. The beginning of his story is so familiar to young black boys. His focus was on sports rather than getting good grades. His athletic ability was phenomenal. He saw that as his meal ticket. His dad urged him not to believe the hype. He stressed the importance of education over athleticism.

Van wasn't trying to hear it. He attended a private school where he became their star athlete on the football team. Football was life. His dad warned him that he wasn't sacrificing to send him to an expensive school and he not get a great education out of it. When Van's grades fell, his dad took him off the football team until he picked them back up. Van made education a priority and succeeded in getting his grades up. He was back on the football team.

Then the unthinkable happened. During a game, Van took a hit that changed his life forever. He described that hit as it being the hit that he wouldn't get back up from. He tried to get up. His entire body felt as if it went to sleep-a tingling sensation like pins and needles. He couldn't move. He was paralyzed from the neck down. Football was over.

Van went from being strong and athletic, to paralyzed and dependent in an instant. Van said he heard his father's voice in his head saying "I told you so"; although his dad never said those words. The rest of his story broke down how he had to be mentally strong, stop asking why and tap into his resilience. Van described himself as always being a hard-worker and having a competitive nature. Those qualities helped him in his journey to regain his mobility. Being relentless, having a relationship with God and having the mentality of "Nobody is going to outwork me" is what go him to where he is today. He ended the session with showing us a picture of himself at physical therapy hoisted up and taking steps to walk. A man that very well could have lived the rest of his life in a hospital bed unable to move, was able to walk.

That part right there is what made the tears want to fall. I wasn't going to let that happen here at this conference full of white nurses and social workers. There were a few sisters, white men and Hispanic women sprinkled in the mix. For the most part, white women were the majority. When folks question if God is real, Van Brooks is a living example that God is the realest. His story was truly inspiring.

I have under an hour to get to Ida B's to meet up with Randy and the crew. I go upstairs to my hotel room and change my clothes from slacks and shoes to jeans and sneakers. I have enough time to walk to the restaurant instead of taking an Uber. It will give me chance to see what's in the area. I quickly tie my laces to my Jordan's, grab my chocolate leather jacket and leave the hotel room.

The walk to the restaurant was interesting. I meet two brothers—one trying to sell me oils, the other asking me to give a small donation in lieu of purchasing the oil. I'm not interested in making a donation or purchasing oil, but I can't knock them for trying. You have to get it how you can get it. At least they ain't out here robbing folks. Instead, they are out here being entrepreneurs.

I make it to Ida B's. I get the same welcoming feeling I got the first time that I visited this establishment. Randy, George and Jerome beat me here. I see them seated at a table in the center of the restaurant. The hostess greets me and I tell her that I see the party I'll be dining with.

"What's good Fellas!" I greet the crew. They all get up to give me a hug.

"Long time no see Boston Buddy." Randy dons me with a new nickname.

"Stop exaggerating. It hasn't been that long."

"Long enough!" Randy says enthusiastically.

"I can't say I've ever heard you refer to something concerning another man being long enough," Jerome says sarcastically.

"Damn fellas, y'all can't keep the conversation decent for longer than one minute I see."

"You know that's right!" Jerome chimes in.

Just as I was about to tell them about the session with Van Brooks, the most stunning women I've ever laid eyes on sits down at our table. I just look at her to see if she's going to say something. She doesn't. Neither does the crew. She picks up her water and sips it before acknowledging me.

"Hi Jean. I'm Imani, Randy's sister."

"Cat got your tongue?" Randy asks. The crew laughs, including Imani.

"Hi. I'm Jean." I say an octave deeper than I needed to. The crew immediately picked up on it.

"Yes, I know your name. I believe I started by saying 'Hi Jean'," Imani says giggling.

"Oh, did you?" I'm distracted by her lips.

She has on lipstick that looks more purple than pink. Her lips look like the red lip emoji on the iPhone. I want to know what those lips feel like against mine. I want those lips wrapped around my dick. If she shows the slightest interest in me tonight, she's getting fucked before I head back to Boston. Sorry Randy. Your sister is dope as hell.

I look at her hand, nothing on the left ring finger. I look back up at her face, but not before looking at her breasts. She is wearing a V-neck fitted black tee-shirt that says YUM in red bold cursive letters across her chest. Yum is right. I imagine she has on a lace bra where I can see the imprint of her nipples. Now, I'm thinking about how those nipples will feel in my mouth.

I'd lick her nipples and drag my tongue up her neck to her succulent lips. I'd kiss her lips then lick them; parting them to taste her tongue. I look at her beautiful eyes and realize that she is staring at me. She's not staring at me in a way of admiration. She's looking at me like she wants to say, "What the fuck are you looking at?" Randy's voice snaps me out of it.

"Damn Jean, did you just fuck my sister at the dinner table, in front of all of us?"

"What? No. Why would you say that? I just have a lot on my mind. Sorry if I seem distracted. Did you say something?" I lie.

"Mmm…I may like men, but I'm still a man. I know what it looks like to undress someone with your eyes. I'm gonna need you to put my sister's clothes back on," He says. As if on cue the table erupts with laughter. Imani looks me directly in my eyes and licks her lips seductively. Then she laughs with the rest of them at my expense. She's just fucking with me. Dinner was a blur. She had me under her spell. I fucked her about four times at the table.

Let me describe this goddess. She's tall. I'd say she's almost six feet. I can tell height runs in her family. Her skin is the same color of my chocolate leather jacket. Her eyes are coal black, they have a slight slant to them. Her nose is sharp with small nostrils. The diamond stud that she has in it is the size of the tip of a ball point pen. It looks like she has thick eye brows but recently got them shaped. Her hair is light brown and dread locked. The dreads are only shoulder length, not down her back like I see a lot of women rocking. I'm assuming her dreads don't have the help of an extension.

Before she sat down, I was able to see just how shapely she is. You know the measurements Q-Tip, from A Tribe Called Quest talks about in in "Bonita Apple Bum" - Yup. All of that. That describes her perfectly. She has on dark blue fitted jeans and what looks like a female version of work boots. Between the yummy top and the tight jeans my x-ray vision already knows what she looks like naked. That's the end game for me. Getting naked with this goddess.

We get ready to leave and I ask her if I could see her again. There's no need to front. The entire table knows that I'm into her. She tells me to give her my number and if she has time she'll hit me up before I head back to Boston. I can't say I've ever been handled in this manner by a woman. I'm not sure how I feel about her response. I have no choice but to oblige or kick rocks. I give her my number.

6

SAVAGE IS AN ADJECTIVE NOT A SYNONYM

Peter:

I was glad to get an unexpected call from Shawn. I need to unwind. After being pulled over by those stereotypical asshole cops, I needed to shake off that feeling of powerlessness it put me in. Shawn's call was right on time. I'm going to meet him at Biff's—the Bury Boys are having a party there. There should be a nice mix of women up in there. I'm in the mood for afro-centric pussy tonight. I'm trying to get into something that won't remind me of white folks tonight. Coming home to a white woman after today's incident fucked with my head.

I tried to talk to her about how I felt, but the shit was so foreign to her. I realized that I was wasting my breath. I guess that is the price you pay when dealing with white chicks. The heart-to-heart conversations focused around the black man's experience are sacrificed. They don't get it, can't get it or won't get it. They can't feel it. I could have talked to Silvie about this. Silvie always got it. Every once in a while, I think about her and how I fucked that relationship up. I had a good thing, but I wanted more than one good thing.

Silvie is a good girl, but she just isn't exciting enough for me. She wanted a story book life. I got tired of hearing about her dreams. That's all they were—dreams. The truth is a black man can't help her with her dreams. It is hard enough for a black man to live a regular life. Every time he opens his eyes in the morning he has to be worried about what bullshit the world is going to throw at him to fuck up his day. Nobody likes the black man. I take that back. Nobody but the black woman likes the black man. That's great for heart-to-hearts and making sure our race doesn't become extinct, but nothing else. The black woman can't do shit for the black man except remind him of all that he can't do for her.

I told Silvie that time and time again. She wasn't buying it. She always talked about "being a stronger force together", "building wealth together", "weathering storms together". I always gave her a good reason why I am not able to do those things with her as a black man. It was like talking to a deaf person that couldn't read lips either. She got pregnant and that added another layer to things. If I stayed with Silvie, not only would I have a life of feeling inadequate as a man, I'd now have the opportunity to feel inadequate as a father. I think she's selfish for even putting me in that position. Her finding out about Patrice was the out that I needed.

I'm at Biff's waiting on Shawn. I'm watching the door as each woman walks in. All types of women are here. The cover for women is free before eleven. It's almost eleven. They are all trying to get in here before they have to pay. Bitches kill me. They don't want to pay to get in or pay to drink. Fuck that. Someone is going to pay with that pussy tonight. Believe that.

This chick sits down beside me at the bar. She looks like she's in here looking for pussy too. She orders gin. She's definitely in here looking for pussy. She is watching the news that's playing on the flat screen TV above the bar. The news is giving some statistics about young black children without the support of their dads. I suck my teeth at the headline. My dyke competition looks at me and asks my opinion.

"What's your take on this?" butch says.

"Trust me. You ain't ready for this conversation," I say dismissing butch.

"Now I really want to know what you think." She sips her gin and gives me her undivided attention. So, I give her something to pay attention to.

"These broads are either keeping the kids from their dads or forcing them on their dads. They knew who they were laying down with. Therefore, they knew what type of a dad he'd be. These females kill me when they act surprised when their new baby daddy acts exactly how he's been acting."

"It sounds like you don't think men should be held accountable," butch questions with her deep ass voice.

"Let's keep it one hundred. If he is an irresponsible dude while you're dating, he'll be an irresponsible dad. If he is cheating on you while you're dating, having a baby isn't going to make him stop. If his money isn't right while you are dating, it damn sure isn't going to be right adding another mouth to feed to the equation."

I finish the rest of my Hennessey and look at her to see if she has something to add. She doesn't. She turns her back to me. Butch is mad disrespectful. How is she just going to turn her back to me? I have more to say. I tap butch on her shoulder. She turns around looking at the shoulder I tapped like I left something on it. I finish my point.

"You gotta admit. Chicks give men too much credit. Stop giving us the benefit of the doubt. Shit would be easier if folks were upfront about their intentions. Chicks be out here making babies with dudes thinking it is going to better their relationship. Some intentionally make a baby, while others get pregnant on accident. Either way it doesn't matter. The moment chicks open their legs to a man raw, you are saying that you are willing to take the risk. You are willing to take what you get. What you get may not be what you dreamt about. You are most likely setting yourself up to get burnt... burnt on every level."

"I've heard enough. You make me glad I only fuck with women. I'm gonna write this off as you being drunk. You can't possibly believe the shit you are talking." Butch is now staring at me like I have something wrong with my face.

"One last point and then I'll leave you alone. You asked for my opinion and now you don't want to hear it. Let me say my piece." Not only is she listening, but the bartender seems entertained by our conversation.

"The point that I am trying to make is that men have gotten used to women being single parents. They have become numb to the shame that should come with not being in your kid's life. I'll admit, I say this because I fall into this category. That's the only way men like me can operate as if we have no conscience; we are numb to it. Men leaving their kids behind for their baby mamas to raise is as common as you hearing about a shooting in the black community. You hear about it. You are not surprised. Then you go back to living your life.

"That is true," the bartender agrees.

"I'm not saying all men are like this. What I am saying is that chicks know what they are getting before they lay down with a dude. They should do a better job picking who they lay down with if they want to make sure that the kid they could potentially be raising is raised right. There are men out there that would make good dads. Those dudes get overlooked." *Dudes like Shawn make good dads. Instead, chicks pick men like me.*

"Yo man, I feel you. These females be in here plotting and be in here crying over the man they plotted on the next week." The bartender sides with me. I decide to wrap this conversation up.

"Females are just as much at fault for all of the kids living in single parent households. Stop being so fucking naïve. Stop thinking that you can change a man. Stop blaming men for their absence. This can be done by not giving them an opportunity to be present in your life from the get go. Women are so fucking starved for attention that they go to bed with anyone that shows them some. As a result, we have generations of kids without their biological dad in the picture. The moms have now transferred their need for attention to the generations of young men that they birthed who will now be starved for male attention. Black women are to blame for the state of the black man."

A few fellas at the bar that were spectating clap as if I just preached the gospel. Butch gives me the finger and leaves the bar.

Shawn walks in and gives me dap once he gets to the bar.

"What is everybody clapping about?" he asks.

"Nothing man. I just had to school somebody and I gained a few fans. That's all," I say laughing.

"Ok. Besides that, what's good Peter?"

"These hoes!" I say laughing.

"I thought you and snowflake were going good."

"We are. When has that ever had anything to do with anything?"

"That's a scary truth. There's always consequences to that," Shawn says as if he's my parent.

"Ain't no consequences with these bitches I can't handle," I say laughing.

"Ok. You're obviously the man. What are you drinking?"

And just like that things were back to normal. Shawn and I had a great night. Butch gave me a little competition when it came to the pussy department, as most men call it, but I got a few numbers to add to my list of pussy outside of Crystal's. He had a little action too. He went home after the party. I didn't. The number that I used tonight didn't disappoint. The sex was so good it made me want to rethink my current living situation.

It's four o'clock in the morning and I'm just getting in. My girlfriend Crystal is up. She has an attitude. She's asking all types of where have you been questions but I shut that shit down immediately. I tell her that I was out with Shawn. She knows that it has been a while since we've kicked it. I don't know why she's tripping. She better go somewhere with that!

Shawn:

Tonight, went as expected. Peter was acting like his normal dog self. Anyone that showed him a little love he tried to set up future dick dates. At first, I was getting worried that he was just going to collect numbers for the night and not follow through with any of them. I should have known better than to worry. Peter is a creature of habit. He left with some young Ethiopian looking woman. She is short, petite and has dreadlocks with silver cuffs on some of them. They look like jewelry for hair. She has light brown skin and round Traci Ellis Ross eyes. Her hair color is jet black. Her eyebrows are too bushy for my liking. Other than that, she's a good-looking girl.

I wait an hour before texting him. My text asks if he saw my license in his car. Meanwhile, my license is in my wallet. Earlier that night, we met at Biff's and had a drink. Then we left together in his car to see what was going on at Slade's. I convinced him it is easier to find one parking spot than two. We stayed there for an hour. We got a plate of their addictive fried chicken and some mac and cheese with yams as sides. When we finished eating, we drove back to Biff's to end our night there. The bouncer recognized us and let us walk back in without carding us. This helped with my plan.

When I texted Peter, I knew that he would be knee deep in the young Ethiopian girl's vagina. Had he not been, he would have responded to my text. After five minutes, I called the house phone looking for him. Crystal answered.

"Hel-lo," she said sleepily. I felt bad for waking her up for bullshit she should have slept through.

"Hi Crystal, it's Shawn. Peter didn't answer his phone? I think I left my license in his car I need him to check. I figured he's not paying attention to his phone. So, I called the house phone. Did he fall asleep that quickly?"

"Hi Shawn. Peter didn't make it home yet. As soon as he does, I'll ask him about your license," I can hear the irritation in her voice.

"Thanks Crystal," I hang up the call.

I didn't leave my license in his car. What I did leave is one of Nakia's earrings on the floor where I was sitting in

Peter's car. I did that just in case Crystal believes whatever lie he comes up with tonight when he comes home. He told me that her car was in the shop but should be out sometime tomorrow. When he gets up to drive her to work, at the Square One Mall, she will notice it where her feet rest. Things at home will change for him whether she confronts him or not. She's going to be suspicious of everything. Things are going to be really uncomfortable for him at home starting now.

My cousin texted me while I was out with Peter. Things are in place. Nakia's sister and brother-in-law's lives will be forever changed as of tomorrow morning. The reporter that she contacted did a little digging of his own and found out even more. Supposedly, this isn't Nakia's sister's first abortion. She's had more than one. The headline's will read: "WIFE OF PRO-LIFE PASTOR ABORTS BABY." This article will cause mass destruction. It will destroy him, his run for candidacy, his marriage and the relationship between Tiffany and Nakia. I guess this is what it means to be a casualty of war.

Elijah:

Sometimes I feel like this dude is stalking me. I'm at Malden Station ready to get settled for the night when I see that idiot Slick that I have to watch my back from. I don't know his real name. We see each other more than I'd like because we run into each other at the shelter. We never speak. We steer clear of each other. He gives me dirty looks and mischievous smiles, but that's about it. He knows better. Nobody starts shit at the shelter because they don't want to be banned from the decent free meals it provides.

Right now, Slick is at the Malden Station in my stall. There is another stall that I could have slept in, but I don't trust him. He is in the stall that I usually sleep in. He's not alone. He's with a chick. Ever see a crack hoe give head to a homeless man? It's an awful sight. It's straight nasty. Think about it. There's no telling when the last time he washed thoroughly. There's also no telling who or what her mouth was on the last time she needed to get high. He's sitting in the stall with her face between his legs slobbering all over his junk.

He sees me coming and doesn't even attempt to stop her. Once I realize that he's getting head, I turn around to shield myself from this horror movie. We briefly make eye contact and this fool smiles at me. Then he busts a nut with no shame or restraint. He does something that I know was an attempt to affect me psychologically. As he is busting his nut he yells "Silvie!" I stop dead in my tracks, but don't turn around. I'll give it to him. He definitely got to me. I guess he figured if he couldn't physically whoop my ass he'd do it psychologically. That was a powerful blow. No pun intended.

I leave Malden Station and just walk. I walk and walk with no destination. I think about how low life can get for some people. That shit right there is casket-low. The chick suffers from addiction. That shit has her doing things her sober self would never consider—but, she's not as bad off as dude. Dude getting head from her is the lost soul. He has clearly settled into this gutter lifestyle.

I don't have a plan B. I'm tired. I'm in the middle of Malden walking around looking suspicious. I need to find somewhere to rest before someone calls the cops on me. I'm really conscious of my appearance and white fear. The last folks I want to run into are the police. I circle back towards the station until I reach the parking garage across the street from Walgreens. I take a chance and go to the top floor stairwell of the garage and sleep there for the night. It's cold, but no colder than it would have been had I slept at Malden Station. I noticed that they have a security guard that drives around. I'm hoping he's too cold to check the stairwell tonight. I'll get as much sleep as I can until he does.

***

I wake up early as usual. My nose is ice cold. The blanket that I had over my face must have fallen. Thank

God, last night was uneventful, but I did have a weird dream which was equally disturbing.

I dreamt Silvie and Slick were a couple. I remember feeling jealous in the dream. Slick was at a black house with a farmer's porch painted red. On the porch were at least twenty anorexic looking prostitutes holding grocery bags full of crack pipes and syringes. They were all wearing red curly wigs that resemble Annie's. They kept passing the bags to each other, swapping crack pipe bags for syringe bags. Every time they passed a bag, something would fall out. Then Silvie appeared. She kept trying to pick up the syringes and pipes the hoes dropped and give them to Slick. Every time she gave them to him, he licked her face. The top layer of his tongue was covered in a thick white substance. It had cracks in it. Between the cracks you could see the flesh of his tongue. It looked like he had a bad case of thrush. I could see this as if I was standing right beside him, except I wasn't. The crazy part about this is that she liked getting licked in the face by this nasty motherfucker.

She would hurry back to the hoes holding the bags to pick up whatever they dropped and bring it back to Slick to get licked some more. Then, unexpectedly, his tongue grew enormously as he licked her face. Pieces of the white layer cracked off as his tongue then wrapped itself around her entire body. It squeezed her like a boa constrictor. I tried to scream to warn her, but nothing came out. It was no use.

She couldn't see or hear me. I woke myself up yelling "Silvie."

I shake off the bad dream and make my way to Planet Fitness. I don't know how I missed the call yesterday, but I had a voice message stating that I have a second interview. They want me to come back in today if possible any time before noon. I'm so glad my grandmother had me iron off a sweater and corduroys while I was visiting her. She then rolled them so that they'd have minimal wrinkles and wouldn't take up a lot of space in my backpack. My interview outfit is in an old Market Basket plastic bag inside of my backpack. The cargo pants and flannel shirt I have on aren't presentable enough to wear to the second interview. I'm glad I'm in Malden still. I walk to Planet Fitness to shower, shave and get dressed.

I'm in and out of Planet Fitness within thirty minutes. My coat is dirty from sleeping in public places on a regular basis. It stinks a little. I'm praying that I don't stink when I take it off. I loaded up on deodorant to the point that it smells like I have on aftershave or a light cologne. I definitely will be removing this coat before I get to the door. There is a parking lot adjacent to the building I'm interviewing at. I'll go in there to remove my coat and walk over without it on. This is what I'm thinking about as I walk to Malden Station.

I reach the station in no time. A familiar face sarcastically greets me.

"Sup Squatter?" I look, but don't say anything.

"I said what's up Nigga?" That got my attention. I mean mug him and reply.

"Your time's gonna be up if you don't get out of my face." He laughs, but I don't.

"Word?"

"Word," I say as if it is a promise.

"Better not let me catch your ass out here sleeping."

I wonder if he means sleeping literally or catching me slipping. I take it to mean both. I always try to do my best not to feed in. He's not the first T-worker to target me. It's not like I don't know how to exhibit self-control and walk away. I do and I've done it. Lord knows that I don't need any additional headaches. Life out here is hard enough. I am not trying to make enemies. I don't need any beef from T-workers. I can already tell that this dude will go out of his way to fuck with me. I walk towards the stairs that lead to the trains.

"So, how you know Silvie?"

I'm shocked. *How does he know Silvie?* He has my undivided attention now. I turn around but say nothing.

"I saw you getting out of her car in front of the station the other day. How you know Silvie? What did you do…con her into giving you a ride? I know her gullible ass would pick up a bum off street."

"It is really none of your business how I know Silvie."

"Oh, I see. You must like her or else you would have continued to keep it moving when I asked the question. You wouldn't have stopped. What? You think she gonna let you hit that? Silvie is a giving woman, but she ain't gonna give it up to no bum that sleeps at train stations. You can forget that," he says snidely.

He hit a nerve with that. He doesn't know it, but that is the very reason why I tried not to entertain any ideas of being with Silvie. He has some sense I see, because he is right. What woman wants a homeless man? I don't bring enough to the table. From what I can assess about this dude testing my patience, neither does he.

"Be careful who you talk shit about. You may need them one day to get you out of some."

I say that and leave. As if it were staged, the train pulls up heading to Forest Hills. I must have shaken a nerve with that one, because he says nothing as I enter the train. Then I hear him yell "niggah please" and the doors close.

I scan the train for an empty spot and take a seat. There are people standing. I wonder why nobody snatched the seat that I am sitting at before I got to it. I'm sitting next to black woman that looks like she is in her twenties, but black doesn't crack, she could be in her fifties. This woman didn't look like a fellow tribe member of the undesirables. That's what I call the homeless. She didn't have body odor from what I could smell. She wasn't talking to herself. Why was this seat not taken? Then her phone rings and I find out why nobody is sitting beside her.

"You think you can fuck with me and get away with it? I know you are behind this shit. Just because I don't want your ass. Look at you! You ain't about shit. You ain't never gonna have shit. Nobody in their right mind would want you for anything more than an orgasm. You fucked me for the last time. And know this, if you fuck with me again I will KILL YOUR BROKE ASS!"

I'm tripping out listening to this woman go off on someone. After her tirade, she sits in her seat in a calm manner and just looks at her phone. That's what she was doing when I sat down beside her. Her phone vibrates a few times indicating that she has a text. It looks like she has several texts. Instead of texting back, she picks up her phone and calls someone. I thought she was going to call the person that was texting her, but she didn't.

"Hey Cuz, I'm gonna need you to fuck somebody up for me."

She's hyped up. Now I see why nobody is sitting next to her.

I try to tune her out. I shut my eyes and replay what just transpired at Malden Station. Dude obviously knows Silvie. As soon as he described her as "giving" I knew he was talking about my Silvie. *Did I just say my Silvie?* I wonder how Silvie knows him. I can't see him being her type. The next time that I see her, I will mention that I met someone that knows her.

I almost miss my stop thinking about how Silvie may know dude. I get off at Downtown Crossing and switch over to the Red Line. I need to get to the Kendall/MIT stop. Where I need to get to is walking distance from the train stop. I stop inside of the parking garage as planned and take off my coat. It's below freezing, but I enter the building coatless. I couldn't risk smelling even a slight bit funky. How you smell, shapes how people think of you and how they interact with you. I'll be damned if I lose a job opportunity over funk.

"Good to see you again Elijah. Thanks for meeting us again under such short notice. I know you must be wondering what this is all about."

"Well, I assumed it was for a second interview," I say careful not to sound sarcastic.

"Well, Elijah, you are right. It is for an interview. Let me begin by letting you know that we offered the job to another candidate."

"I guess I'm a little confused," I say with a blank face, but I really want to drop a tear.

"We didn't feel that you were a good fit for that position. As a company, we are trying to grow in many areas. We are trying to be innovative and progressive. We want to continue to be a leader in this sphere. We do feel that you would be a great fit for a position that we've been wanting to create. How would you like to be the Director of Patient Relations? You'd be working with the patient advocacy groups and patient foundation groups. You'd also be responsible for collecting data regarding how patients feel about their relationship with us. The salary is double of what we were offering for the position you applied for."

All I heard was double the salary. I spent the next two hours filling out paper work. Meeting people and touring the building. Today is turning out to be one of my best days of life. Once I did the math, I realized that the salary, for this position, is over a hundred grand a year. I am going from making seventy-five dollars a day to one hundred and ten thousand a year! My grandmother always told me that God will exceed your expectations if you wait on him. Thank you, God! What I didn't know is that they also offered a five-thousand-dollar sign on bonus. My cup runneth over!

That will definitely be enough for first and last deposit to rent an apartment. It's funny how life can change for you in an instant. Some months ago, I was put out on the street with no girlfriend, no job and nowhere to go. Today, I am offered the highest paying job I've ever had. See how God works. I'm so ready to get some stability in my life. I've been craving it. Today is supposed to be a snow storm. I don't even care at this point. No storm can ruin my high right now. God is good all the time.

It's going to be too cold to sleep outside. I planned on staying at the shelter tonight, but since I will now be generating some serious income, I'm not going to the shelter tonight. I'm going to rent a room for a few nights. I'll shovel all day today and tomorrow to make some of that money back. I can't wait to tell my grandmother!

Peter:

Ok. So, I promised God that I'd be a better boyfriend. I already fucked up and cheated. Being a better boyfriend is going to take time. I'm not doing too well in that department so I decide to follow through on my next promise. I start working on being a better father immediately. I call Silvie.

"Hello," she says after the third ring.

"Hey where's my son?" I question Silvie.

"Well, hello to your rude ass too," she says with an attitude and doesn't answer my question.

"My bad Silvie. I'm just in a rush to get to work, but I wanted to make sure I spoke to you before I left."

"Mmm hmm, " Silvie says as if she's not buying it.

"Ok, let me start over. Hi Silvie! Is my son home?" I say sarcastically.

"Yes. What can I do for you?

"I'd like to see him Saturday if that's ok."

"I'm sure that can be arranged. Depending on the time. You know that I volunteer at the shelter on Saturday and your son spends time with his Uncle Jean while I'm there."

"Well, his Uncle Jean is gonna have to give up his Saturday this week. He don't need to be around your hating ass brother so much any way."

"First of all, you're not going to speak of my brother in a negative light. Second, you don't spend any time with your son. You need to thank my brother for being the consistent male presence in his life," Silvie says. She sounds like she is rolling her neck as she tries to put me in my place.

"Look, can I see my son on Saturday, or not?" I say agitatedly.

"I'll drop him off to you before I go to the shelter. Are you still at the same address or did your white girlfriend give you your walking papers? I just want to make sure I am going to the right address. I didn't know if Shawn's house is your residence again."

"You always find a way to slide some bullshit into our conversation. Yes. I am still at the same address. I am still living with Crystal."

"Great. I'll drop him off before I go to the shelter and then pick him up when I'm done."

"That sounds good. What time is that?"

"I'll text you what time I'll be there. I'm usually done within five hours."

"Ok, I can handle that. Five hours should fly by. I'll see you then."

And just like that it was done. She didn't really give me a hard time about wanting to spend some time with my son after all this time. I hope he doesn't whine about wanting to be with his mother. I mean, he is with her most of the time. It would make sense if he wanted to go home early. I just hope that he gives me a chance to get to know him. I know it's been a long time since I spent any time with him.

Hopefully, I can start making up for lost time. I plan on making good on my promise to God. He got me out of a jam. I promised to be a better man, father and boyfriend. I'm going to start with being a better father. That'll trickle down and make me a better man. Consider me a work in progress for being a better boyfriend. That's going to take some serious work or it'll take a woman that is down with an open relationship.

I grab my lunch, my keys and head out to work. Things are looking up. I think about what Oliver and I will do on Saturday. It's too cold to go to the park. Maybe, we can go to Sky Zone or something. Maybe we can go to a movie. Then we can grab a pizza and eat it while we wait for Silvie to pick him up. I wonder if he likes video games. I'll let him play a few of my games and see if he takes a liking to it. Whatever it is, I want to spend time with him by myself.

I'm going to have to find a way to get Crystal out of the house for few hours. I'll give her some dick and then pay for her to get her hair done. That should buy me a few hours to bond with my son. I hope. It's time like these I wish I had my own spot. I hear the voices of Shawn and Silvie in my head. Both of them have told me that I need to get my own spot. The truth is, I like the flexibility of not owning the place or having to sign a lease. If I want to bounce I can. Shawn and Silvie have it wrong. They think I'm dependent on the woman because she has the place in her name. What they don't see is that I'm liberated by it.

My phone vibrates. It's Silvie. She texted me and asked if it is ok to drop Oliver off early. She'd like to do some grocery shopping before going to work her shift at the shelter. I texted her back and said no problem. Looks like we are going to have a full day together. I wonder if she's going to feed him before she drops him off. I'm tripping. I know Silvie. She's going to assume that I am not going to be prepared. She'll feed him. I'll take care of lunch and snack.

Now that Oliver is coming earlier, I am going to have to get Crystal out of the house for sure. I'll tell her that I am sorry for the other night. Give her some money to get her hair and nails done. On second thought, that is not going to give me enough time. If Crystal was a black woman, that would give me the entire day. White hair salons don't take as long as the black ones. I'm going to have to give her some money to go to the mall shopping. Shit. I'm not trying to waste all of my money on her. I need some money to spend on my son.

I decide to give Crystal money to get her hair and nails done. That's it. By the time she comes back, Oliver and I will be out and about. I'm going to apologize tonight. I'll cancel my plans with my Ethiopian shorty and stay home with Crystal. I'll give her some dick and tell her that I want to make things up to her. I'll have her feeling good tonight and looking forward to her "me time" tomorrow. Plant that dick and then plant the seed, that's all it'll take. I'm still not sure how or where I slipped up, but she is on to me. I could have seen my new shorty tonight and had Crystal out of the house early if I had not have made her suspicious. Oh, well. Shorty ain't going anywhere. I'll see her tomorrow night after work.

Elijah:

I agreed to start my new job on Monday. There was no need to waste time. I am ready to begin this new phase of my life. I'm not only going to be able to take care of myself, but I'm going to be able to take care of somebody else if need be. I'm so fucking excited! I spend a big part of my morning daydreaming.

Last night, I rented a room at the Days Inn on route one in Saugus. They had a room for $99 a night. I was beat after all the shoveling that I did last night. It felt so good to have a clean spot to myself for a few nights. I was able to take long hot shower in and masturbate in peace. I could use the private bathroom without rushing. I could wear one layer of clothing and be comfortable. Shit. I could turn the heat up and wear just my briefs if I wanted to. More importantly, I could leave my bag unattended. I could watch TV if I wanted, although I enjoy reading books more. The point is that I could if I wanted to. I could do pretty much whatever with the luxury of not having to watch my back. Spending the night at the hotel made me want my own apartment even more. It became an urgency.

I empty out the contents of my backpack. My entire life is in this backpack. A scratch ticket falls out. *There it is.* I only gave my grandmother one scratch ticket with her birthday card. I was too embarrassed to empty out my bag to dig for the second scratch ticket. So, she only got one. It became a non-issue when she hit one hundred bucks off the scratch ticket. She was so hyped about it. I believe she did the elderly version of the cabbage patch dance. I was cracking up!

I dig in my bag for change. My grandmother believes that you must scratch tickets with a penny. I always tell her that the numbers on the ticket aren't going to change based on what you scratch it with. She is adamant that it matters whether or not you use the penny but gives no explanation behind it. I honor her custom and find a penny in my bag. The two numbers that I need to match are six and thirteen. I have ten chances to match my numbers. The card reads if I get a dollar sign I can multiply the total winnings times ten. The first number is a thirteen. The second number is a thirteen and all the rest are the number six. Generally, the numbers six and thirteen tend to be unlucky numbers. In my case, those numbers are my new lucky numbers.

I win one thousand dollars on each number. That is ten thousand dollars! My heart rate speeds up. A feeling of warmth wraps itself around me like a blanket when I scratch the area to find out if I'll get a dollar sign. When I scratch the dust away from the scratch off, I can't believe my eyes. I just won ten times ten thousand dollars!

Tears begin to cloud my sight. They begin to pour out wetting every pore in my face. I'm crying tears of joy. I am crying tears of relief. I drop to my knees and thank God. I was put in a position where I lived with just the necessities of life and sometimes less than that. Now look at what God did! I'm seeing the fruits of all those uncomfortable nights that I praised God despite my circumstances. Every night I'd say *"God you are in control. I know you can change my circumstances."*

Today, God is putting me in a position to fulfill my wants and needs. I have to wait until Monday to cash in my ticket. Since it is such a large amount, I have to go to the lottery office in Woburn to cash the ticket. Had it been less money, I could have gone straight to the liquor store to cash it. You'll hear no complaints from me. These are the kind of problems I don't mind having. Instinctively, I map out my next move aligning it with the MBTA schedule. *Forget that. I'm taking Uber.* I smile as I think about this journey that is no more. I've spent my last night on the street.

As I put on my clothes to head to the shelter, I think about Silvie. I can't wait to take her out to dinner. I can't wait to spend more time with her. There are so many things I want to do with her. Had my ex-girlfriend not put me out, I wouldn't have met Silvie because I wouldn't have been at a shelter. Had my ex-girlfriend showed some compassion and not put me out on the street I wouldn't have walked into the store where the white man cut me in line and ignored me when I spoke up about it. Had that white man had a heart, he would have acknowledged me and he would have gotten his bag returned to him. Had this happened, had that happened, at the end of the day, God's plan was so much more intricate than I could have ever thought up for myself. The lesson in all this...*trust God.*

Since I didn't care about getting to the shelter in time to get a meal, I was late getting there. I honestly just wanted to be there to help the ladies clean up and ask Silvie out on a date. One of the ladies that cooks smiles at me when she sees me walking towards her.

"We thought you and Silvie were skipping out of work today. Glad to see you made it. I made a plate for you and put it to the side. I know that is what Silvie would have done had she showed up today."

"She's not here?" I ask with disappointment in my voice.

"Nope, she no showed. No call and no show. Which isn't like her. She didn't answer her phone when I called. Hope she's not sick. Now that I think of it, even if she was sick, she would have called. Dear Lord, I hope she's ok."

"You wouldn't happen to have her address, would you? I know what street she lives on but I don't know the number address," I ask as worry begins to consume me.

"Elijah had you asked me for her address on any other day, I wouldn't have told you. It would be wrong of me, but something doesn't feel right. I know Silvie cares about you and you care for her. Privacy has to be thrown out the door when safety is questioned. She lives on …."

***

As soon as she gave me the number address, I went on my Uber app and set up a ride. I apologized that I would not be able to help them clean up today. I have to make sure Silvie is alright. I start praying silently. My eyes are closed, but they open when I smell something that interrupts my prayer. The smell is aggressive because it's standing right in front of me. It's Slick. He could have had the drop on me, but again, he doesn't want to get kicked out of the shelter.

He looks at me and smiles. His smile is comical and equally sinister. It looks like he only has a total of ten teeth in his mouth. The ones that I can see are yellow and rotting. At this moment, I remember the dream that I had with him in it. The Uber driver pulls up as I stand outside with this creature in front of me. He says nothing. I walk away and head towards the car. As I'm getting in he yells to me.

"The pussy was better than I expected."

I shake my head as I get into the car. *Is this fool crazy?* I don't even respond. Why he would think that I would give two shits about him getting some from one of his crack hoes is beyond me. I really need to just bust this dusty negro in his mouth. Some people don't see the error in their ways until someone fucks them up. Then they get the picture.

I try to shake thoughts of beating this fool's ass and direct my thoughts to the next moves I am going to make once I get this money. The Uber driver speaks. He's not on the phone and I am the only one in the car. It is safe to assume that he is talking to me.

"What you give in life is what God reimburses you. Your friend doesn't seem to have learned that yet. I will pray that he finds his way before he becomes lost."

I let those words marinate. For the rest of the trip he says nothing. He doesn't try to make small talk. He just drives in silence. When he does speak it is powerful and impactful.

"Holbrook St," The Uber driver announces as if he's announcing train stops.

I thank him for the ride and the wisdom. I also add that the dude he is referring to is not my friend. I get out of the car and shut the door. He rolls down his passenger side window.

"He may not be your friend, but he is your brother. His problems are our problems. He is you, minus a few bad decisions, circumstances and agents of socialization. Keep him in your prayers too, Brother."

That shit hit home. It was something that I didn't want to hear nor expect to hear. But it was the truth. The truth is often hard to swallow.

I enter Silvie's building as someone is coming out. This allows me access to the staircase that leads to her door. She lives on the third floor of this multi-family apartment building. As I walk up the stairs my heart races. It's not because the stairs are working me. It is because I'm not sure how she is going to react when she sees me. I'm hoping that she is happy to see me. My pace slows down as I begin to wonder if I have crossed a line by coming here. I just want to check on her and make sure that she is ok. A lot of people have been coming down with the flu. People that have gotten their flu shot have come down with the flu. Like I said, I just want to make sure she is ok.

I reach the top floor. There are only two apartments to each floor. They are separated by the staircase. I read the number on the door to my left and to my right. Her number is on my right. There's loud music playing in her neighbor's apartment. As if on cue, I hear Rick Ross "When you black, lips chapped, cause the game cold."

I knock on Silvie's door. I listen to see if I hear any movement. Nothing. I knock again and wait. Nothing. I turn around and walk to the hallway window. You can see the building's parking lot. I look to see if Silvie's car is there. I don't expect to see it because she didn't answer the door, but I look anyway.

There it is. Her car is here. That means she is here or her car is not working. I knock on her door again a little louder this time with more force behind it. Something tells me to check the door to see if it is locked. I turn the knob and it's unlocked. I open the door wide and leave it open. I don't even get a chance to admire her furnishings because I am blown away by a familiar sickening smell. I walk further into the apartment and what I see next breaks my heart.

Silvie is tied to a dining room chair naked. The chair is on its back instead of its legs. Her legs are tied with rope. Her hands are tied behind the chair with rope and her mouth is taped shut. *How did she get on her back?* I rush over to her to see if she is breathing. She's breathing, but she is unconscious. There's blood in her hair. She must have a gash somewhere. I find a blanket and cover her body while I call 911 and opt not to remain on the line. I look around for her pocketbook. When the paramedics get here, they will have questions. I find it in her bedroom. I take out her keys. I find her wallet with her driver's license and health insurance card. I pack a bag for her. She'll be in the hospital overnight. She has a bible on the nightstand. I pack that too. There's a picture of her son Oliver on the same night stand. I figure she'll be comforted by this when she wakes up. When I hear the buzzer I rush to the door. It's the paramedics. I let them in. The police arrive next.

7

JEZEBEL WAS A VICTIM

Peter:

Silvie should have been here by now. I know that Oliver is with his dad, but damn, she hasn't even checked on him since he has been with me. Pretty soon, I'm going to go over her place and see what the holdup is. Don't get me wrong, I'm enjoying my time with Oliver. It feels like she is trying to teach me a lesson or something. If she isn't here by 8pm. I'm going to her place to drop him off. I have shit to do and I have to get up early for work in the morning.

***

It's 8:30pm. I'm ringing Silvie's buzzer and she isn't answering. My son and I get back into the car and drive around to the back. Her car isn't in the parking lot. This chick is running the streets. She is so fucking irresponsible. She dropped our son off early this morning so that she could do some grocery shopping. She can't still be at the shelter. Why isn't she answering her phone. She plays too many games for me.

I take Oliver back to my house to see if she is waiting for us there. Maybe something is up with her phone. Crystal isn't home yet. I'm relieved, but I'm also wondering where the hell she's been all day. Oliver asks if he is sleeping over. He says that he is sleepy. I get some blankets and prepare a place for him on the couch. He's young. It's probably past his bedtime. I don't even know what his bedtime is. I put him to sleep and then start thinking about how I'm going to cuss his mother out when she gets here. She's probably laid up with some dude somewhere. I fall asleep on the recliner mad.

I can't believe this broad. It's seven o'clock in the morning. I thought that she was different, but I see she is just like the other baby mama's out there. She'll use her kid to get back at her baby's daddy. These females don't think about how their immature behavior is going to affect the kid. If they do think about it, they must think that it is worth the sacrifice.

Silvie didn't call or come by and Crystal didn't come home. What the fuck is up with bitches lately? They want to act up at the same time. I am supposed to be to work in thirty minutes. That can't happen unless….

I call Silvie's brother Jean to see if he has heard from her and if he could possibly come scoop Oliver up. He doesn't pick up his phone. I call Crystal to see where the fuck she's at and she doesn't pick up either. Silvie still isn't answering the phone. It's like she left me to babysit indefinitely. I call my job to let them know that I can't make it in. I'm pissed at this point. Oliver is still asleep. He's going to be hungry when he wakes up. Crystal isn't here to make us any breakfast. Hope we got some milk or else he'll be having dry cereal this Sunday morning.

Shawn:

I'm listening to Urban View's Karen Hunter Show. Her guest speaker is Dr. Tony Van Der Meer. He's a professor at UMASS Boston. They are discussing the relationship between black men and black women in the United States. This brother makes some good points.

"This is Karen Hunter and you are listening to the Karen Hunter Show on Sirius Urban View. If you are just tuning in, we are here with my guest Dr. Tony Van Der Meer. He's a professor of

Africana Studies at UMASS Boston. So, let's dive right back in. The last caller I had to cut short because on the Karen Hunter Show we are all about solutions, not problems. He made a point to say he's tired of black women and their whining. He said we complain too much about black men as if black women have it all together. He said that he's surrounded by plenty of black women that make black men their scapegoat. Had I not cut him off, what would you have said to him Professor?"

"I would ask the question: How did he come to that conclusion and what other factors, that may have bene instrumental, help to shape his understanding of what the problem is."

"Come on Professor! Is that all you'd say? With all that knowledge I know you have, you wouldn't hit him off with some facts?"

"Sorry Karen, but I'd continue to ask questions. As Amiri Baraka would say, 'when you ask why, you will get wise.' Then, I'd ask the caller how many women are in the world? What is the percentage of the women he has experience with versus those he doesn't. Then I would ask is his view a subjective or an objective view.

Let's explore what social standards are set for the kinds of relationships we encounter and develop for ourselves. Black people are living in a world governed by others who have shaped how we see ourselves and them. How do you balance that with the psychology of oppression and the ideology of white supremacy that have marginalized Black men and women into accepting their own racial, gender and class inferiority?"

"Yes Dr. Van Der Meer! That's how you let him know that you have letters after your name! Let's take the next caller."

As if on cue, my phone rings.

"Hello."

"You couldn't just be sad for a minute and then move on! You had to go to the next level and make sure you hurt me. You knew you couldn't hurt me because I don't give a fuck about you or what you are doing. So *you* decide to hurt me through my family. I'll give it to you. That was clever of you. You made it so I didn't have no choice but to give a fuck. You have my attention now Shawn, but you know something? You ain't never going to have me. Your dead-beat friend had more game than you. That's why he got it. You might want to take some lessons from him. He may be a piece of shit, but he got a Safaree dick. Who am I talking to? Your lame ass doesn't watch *Love and Hip Hop*."

I hit her with a long awkward pause. She's expecting me to be combative. No need to. I see I've already won. All I wanted was for her to feel pain. She needed to feel uncomfortable with life. By her calling me, she confirms that life is officially uncomfortable. Life blindsided her. Life backhanded her. I wish her nothing, but stress, stress and more stress. Not only will she be stressed, but she won't have her sister, her confidante, to vent to. She's going to have to cope by herself…just like I did.

"What the fuck! Say something! Are you stuck on stupid or something? Oh, you ain't got shit to say huh,

Shawn? That's just like you to be passive aggressive. Why am I surprised? You know my sister isn't talking to me because of you Shawn. My sister hates me because of you! You silent now, but your big mouth had a lot to say to the paper. Because of YOU, my sister's husband chose his congregation over his marriage. Because of YOU, he is divorcing my sister. Did you hear me? He is divorcing my sister because of some shit that you started. This is all because your bitch-ass couldn't get over a break-up. Instead, you try to ruin a couple's marriage which had absolutely nothing to do with our situation. That's childish, stupid and dangerous. Know this Shawn. This shit ain't over. If you think you can drag my family's name through the mud, you are mistaken! You might have thought that this stunt made us even, but you are wrong. It's on."

"Is that supposed to scare me?" I'm talking to myself because she abruptly hangs up. One down and one more to go. I'm tired of people thinking that they can hurt me and not expect there to be consequences. If you hurt me. I'm going to hurt you. Period. There's only one person that got away with hurting me, but nobody since then. So, If Nakia wants to continue this game, she's going to learn very quickly that I come from a family that doesn't play for fun. We play to win or destroy.

I've always felt conflicted about hurting the first and last person that got away with hurting me. By hurting them, I felt I'd be hurt all over again. It's complicated. How do you tell your best-friend that his older sister molested and raped you? I couldn't tell my mother either. Believe me. I debated with myself about telling her. When I saw how she reacted to Peter's situation, I knew my disclosure would only make things more complicated. I just wanted to forget about it and be done with it. I stopped going to Peter's house after I was raped by his sister. Shortly after, Peter started living with us. This shielded me from ever having to explain why I didn't want to go to his house anymore.

Peter's mom worked nights. She had to be to work by 3pm and got off at 11pm. This meant that she only got to interact with her son in the morning before school and on weekends. His older sister, Donna, had to babysit Peter until their mom arrived from work. Donna was expected to make sure Peter was in the house by 8pm. She had to make sure that he ate, did his homework and was in bed by 10pm. This limited her free time.

We were in eighth grade. Donna was in the tenth grade. She always had an attitude because she couldn't hang out with her friends during the week outside of her home. Her girlfriends could come over, but they had to leave by 7pm, an hour before Peter's curfew. I remember Donna as being bossy as hell. You would have thought that Peter was her son rather than her brother.

It was a Wednesday night. Peter and I were in the living room playing video games. There was food in the house, but there was nothing to snack on. Peter had some weed that he wanted to smoke. He didn't want to be without snacks when his munchies kicked in. The corner store was three blocks away. He told me to sit tight and he'd be back. I offered to go with him, but he said he was going to holler at the Dominican girl who worked there. Her family owned the store. He didn't need me messing things up for him. He said he'd be back in fifteen minutes or less. I stayed put and played the video game.

Donna walked into the living room. It was only 7pm and she was dressed for bed. She had on an oversized red t-shirt doubling as a nightgown and fuzzy black socks. She usually pays me no attention. I think she felt as if I was just another kid that she had to babysit. As she approached the couch, she ordered me to press pause on the game. She said that she wanted to see something on TV. It was her house. As much as I didn't want to get off of the game, I did as I was told.

She popped in a DVD and I decided to leave. I got up to head to Peter's room and wait for him. She tells me that I didn't have to leave. She told me to sit with her and wait for her brother. He's only been gone for about five minutes at this point. When the movie comes on, I see a woman on all fours taking it from the back. Her breast are being squeezed by the man giving it to her doggy style. She is moaning like she's really enjoying herself.

"You like that huh?" Donna asked.

How was I supposed to respond to that? I was embarrassed to be watching this movie and more so because I was with my best friend's sister. She asked me again, but this time her hand was on my dick. I tensed up. I was frozen. I didn't even know if I was breathing. My mind was telling me to get up and leave, better yet run. Unfortunately, the way Donna's stroked my dick it was hard to get up and leave. I don't know what to do. I've masturbated plenty of times, but I never had anyone else stroke my dick besides me. It felt good, but something inside of me kept telling me to get up. It felt wrong. It was wrong. What does a tenth grader want with an eighth grader?

I gathered as much strength as I could and got up. She stood in front of me and asked if I was a bitch that didn't like pussy. Until that day, I never had pussy. I thought it was a trick question. I knew that once I got some pussy, I liked it, but I didn't want any from her. Donna wasn't trying to hear it. She pushed me back down onto the couch. Then she straddled me. I was so nervous. You heard it in my voice as I asked her to stop.

"You know you want this pussy." She lifted up her t-shirt which left her naked underneath.

"I need to go." I pleaded with her in a whisper.

"You ain't going nowhere," she said as she unbuttoned my jeans.

"Peter will be here in any minute. You better get off me," I said in a panic. I hoped that this would have gotten her off me.

"I told Peter to pick me something up from the Chinese food spot. I just called my order in. So, we got at least another fifteen minutes before he comes back."

"Look, you're a pretty girl, but I really don't want to do this Donna. Peter wouldn't like this either," I again pleaded with her.

Donna smiled and then kissed me. Her breath stunk. I locked my lips. I knew that I was stronger than her. I should have been able to get her off me. Why couldn't I?

This was the first time that I experience myself jump out of myself and watch as if I was someone else. Donna kept telling me that people would think I was gay if I didn't fuck her. She said that she would spread a rumor that I liked dick instead of pussy. She warned that I wouldn't want that reputation going into high school that September. I still protested, but it was too late.

Donna managed to pull my dick out and sit on it raw. I was taught in school that when two people have sex, they are supposed to use a condom. I remembered the pictures of what can happen to your genitalia if you catch a sexually transmitted disease. I sat there, still. Her thighs had me in a grip. I was afraid. I did nothing. Peter's sister fucked and forced me to watch porn while doing so. She was bouncing up and down faster and faster. The harder she bounces, the harder she breathe. Her breath smelled like trash. I want her off me.

She was moaning and so was the white woman in the video. I couldn't see Donna's face, but I could see the white couple's faces. They were loving it. Was I supposed to be loving it too? The moaning combined with Donna's wet pussy made me bust a nut within two minutes flat. I began moaning. That must've meant I liked it. Right? I was so confused. What just happened? Whatever happened, I sure didn't see it coming.

Donna got off me. She wiped me off and put my dick back in my pants. She fixed my clothes back up as if what just went down never went down. Five minutes later Peter came back. I told him that I had to go home because my mom needed me to do something. It was a lie, but I had to get out of there. Since then, I have never went back. She's the last person that I let hurt me. I'm convinced that the Jones' raised demons instead of children. Donna and Peter are evil beings.

Elijah:

The tip of my nose feels cold. I don't realize that the rim of my nostril is wet until it starts to itch. I instinctually wipe my nose with my sleeve. I regret it as soon as I do it. Now my sleeve has snot on it. I get up from my seat and walk to the area where the plastic gloves, gowns and masks are kept. Tissues are also there. I grab a few to wipe my nose, something I should have done from jump. I wipe the snot off of my sleeve but there is still evidence of mucus on it.

I sit back down in the uncomfortable hospital room chair. *Why do they have it so cold in here?* I look over at Silvie who is now sleeping. They gave her something to calm her down. When she became conscious she was hysterical. I was relieved that she woke up when she got here, but I'm glad she went back to sleep. She had to be mentally exhausted from all the questioning the detective put her through. The police officer that came in to take her statement coerced her to talk. It seemed like Silvie didn't want to.

I didn't understand her reluctance. If somebody violated me, I'd be eager to tell the police. I'd be fixated on the police catching the person. It wasn't until they mentioned her son Oliver that she started to cooperate. They asked her where her son was at the time of the assault and asked where he is now. They wanted to know if she had a plan for his care while she is in the hospital.

She has a nasty bump on her head, but the doctor said she'll be ok. She has a concussion. The female detective urged her to allow the hospital to perform a rape kit on her. Silvie agreed to it. After it was performed, the nurses went back to their station. I overheard two nurses talking. They didn't say her name, but I knew that they were talking about Silvie. They felt bad for her. According to them, the rapist did a number on her. They were talking about how swollen she was down there.

Never piss off a nurse. They are the masters of creative ways to inflict cruel and unusual punishment. The tall, heavy-set, nurse with the short wig and Jamaican accent said that somebody should take a pencil and shove it up the rapist's penis, like a catheter. She didn't stop there. Then she added that once the pencil is lodged in place, that same person should take two bricks and slam them shut on his penis causing the pencil to break inside of him. The pale, skinny, red head nurse assigned to Silvie's room laughed and said, "let's see him try to get those splinters out." I cringed as they howled with laughter.

After they finished interviewing Silvie, she started to fade off to sleep. I sat there as she fell asleep. I'm not going anywhere tonight. I'll be sleeping right in this chair. I don't want her to feel like she is alone. When she wakes up, whenever that is, I'll be here for her.

I open the Bible that I took off her night stand and I decide to start reading 2nd Corinthians 4:8. It's my nana's favorite. It must be Silvie's too, because there is a white piece of paper folded up like a bookmark holding its place. Curiosity gets the best of me. I unfold the paper. I can't imagine what it is.

I'm looking at something that makes no sense. It doesn't make sense because it contradicts what Silvie told me. Silvie has no reason to lie to me. What I'm reading basically confirms that Silvie lied to me and a few other people. I fold the paper back up and place it right back where I found it in Corinthians. Right now, the only thing that is important is Silvie's recovery.

Love is patient. Love is kind.

I think about what I just read. *Who is Tyson Brown?* The name that should be beside the numbers 99.999 percent is Peter. I read it three time before I put it back inside of her Bible. *Why did she lie?* I'm trying not to judge, but it's hard not to. I can't ask her. I'm not even supposed to know. I would have never known had I not been nosey and went through her Bible. I wasn't in there snooping with hopes of finding a deep dark secret. That's exactly what I found.

Peter isn't Oliver's biological father....

***

I wake up from a nap that I didn't know I took. I have no idea what time it is, but it must be after midnight. The corridor is quiet. There's not a lot of movement going on out there. I hear the machine that monitors Silvie's vital signs. She is sitting up. The television is on, but the volume is muted. Silvie has her Bible in her hands. It's open. She's holding the piece of paper that holds the truth, on top of the Bible, instead of inside of it. Now she is looking at me.

"So, you know," she says in a soft sad voice.

I pause before answering. I could simply say yes, but she deserves more than that. She's hurting on so many levels. I don't want to add to it by answering in a way that may inflict guilt or sound like disappointment. Instead of answering yes, I say, "I'm here for you." At this time, this is what she needs to hear. She needs to know that I won't be another man that leaves her when the times get hard. She is sobbing. It's coming from somewhere deep. She cries tears filled with years of heartache, feelings of abandonment and I can only imagine whatever else. I hold her close. So, close that her tears become mine as they roll down my cheek. When the tears stop. She tells me her story.

"The first time that I was pregnant by Peter, he begged me to abort it. Believe me. I didn't want to, but I didn't think that I was strong enough to raise a child alone. He warned me that he wasn't in a position to provide for a child. He told me to use my common sense. At the time, us having a child together wasn't a good idea. Peter had a crafty way of flipping things around. Something could be his fault entirely. By the time we finished arguing, what was once his fault, was now mine. He made me feel irresponsible for even considering keeping the baby. So, I aborted it."

She wipes tears from her eyes trying to keep it together. I reach over to her bedside table and hand her some tissues. I want to hug her but I know she needs to tell the rest of her story.

"I'm sorry Silvie. I know that must have been a hard decision to make." She takes a deep breath and then continues.

"The second time that I got pregnant, I told him that I was keeping it. There was no way I was going to have another abortion. By this time, I already knew where he stood. Right before I found out that I was pregnant, I had my suspicions about Peter cheating on me. I swear, I could feel it, but I couldn't prove it. So, I did things I'm not proud of just so I could feel like he wasn't getting over on me."

My facial expression must have involuntarily changed because Silvie straightens up and sits erect, like she's testifying in court.

"During my first trimester is when I got the proof. He was at my apartment in a drunken sleep. He had gotten into the bad habit of staying out late with no explanation of his whereabouts. Since he didn't want to be forthcoming with where he'd been, I decided to check his phone. Usually, I respect people's privacy. My respect for Peter had become minimal and his respect for me had become nonexistent. He fell asleep on his stomach. His phone was in his back pocket. His right arm was hanging off the bed. I slid the phone out of his pocket and used his thumb to unlock it. I feared that Peter was just another man that was going to be added to my long list of disappointments. The pictures and text messages in his phone confirmed that my gut was right. I was a fool."

"You weren't a fool. He was a piece of shit."

"Well, I sure felt like one Elijah. I wasn't the only person that he got pregnant. There was another woman having my man's baby. I remember feeling another piece of my already fractured and fragile heart, break. Call it what you want. Some call it naive but I'm a woman that believes that as long as you have breath, you can change."

"I share the same belief Silvie." I want to reach out and hug her.

"I'd hoped that maybe Peter would come around and embrace the idea of becoming a dad. That hope died once I learned that he had another woman pregnant. I knew the likelihood of him embracing fatherhood was slim to none. He made it clear that he didn't want to be a dad. Now, he would be fathering two children. Peter was proving me wrong. He not only still had breath, but he was sucking the life out of me, with no signs of change to come."

I stop her. "You don't have to continue if this is too hard to relive. I appreciate you telling me as much as you have." I can't see her sad. Her eyes look sad. I felt sorry for Silvie. Listening to this was hard. It was hard not to hate Peter.

"No. I want to finish. I want to put everything on the table."

"Ok Silvie. I'm all ears." I nod my head encouraging her to keep going.

"All the things that I didn't like about him or our relationship hit me at once. It was a heavy—handed blow. The many things that I forgave him for, I replayed over and over in my mind. He didn't deserve forgiveness. As he laid asleep on my bed, I thought about how comfortable he looked. Then I thought about how uncomfortable he's made my life.

He lived with me but didn't pay any rent. He said if it was the other way around he wouldn't dare ask me to pay rent. He often asked me to charge things on my credit card for him. When I did, instead of him paying off the balance, he only paid the minimum. Sometimes he didn't pay that. Then the minimum balance got so high that he couldn't keep up with it. Let's just say that my credit score dropped substantially because of him.

One night as he was sleeping, I thought about where he'd go if I kicked him out. As dumb as this sounds, I still cared about him, despite what he did to me. It was like I had a disease that caused me to think of his feelings before my own. Then his phone beeped indicating that he had a text. It was from Patrice. The woman that was pregnant too. It said that she had a wonderful night. And thanks again for paying her rent. That $500 really helped her out. I remember becoming enraged learning that information. He paid her rent! He never contributed a dime here because he always cried broke. He had money to pay her rent though. And whose rent is only $500? I remember thinking that she must have Section 8 subsidized housing."

"If I only had to pay $500 for rent I wouldn't be homeless," I say laughing. Silvie laughs with me.

"I woke him up to let him know that his other baby mama was texting him. I told him that he had a half of an hour to gather his belongings and get the hell out of my house. He could go live with Patrice, since he was already paying rent there."

"I hear you," I say agreeing wholeheartedly.

"From that point on, I called myself trying to make him be more responsible. He never really bonded with Oliver. Since I couldn't make him be a dad, I wasn't going to let him off the hook with having to support his son monetarily. He was going to pay. I told him that if he didn't help me, I'd go to court to put him on child support. I knew that Patrice already had him on child support. He didn't want any more court involvement. He agreed to pay me in cash regularly.

Payments have been anything, but regular. They are consistently inconsistent and they vary in amount. It wasn't until a year after Oliver was born that I found out that Peter wasn't his biological father. Peter never spent time with Oliver. If I told him that Peter wasn't his son, he would have only been upset that he paid child support for a child that wasn't his. He couldn't complain about a bond that he never built. Peter put me in a lot of debt. I still had credit cards that were maxed out that he stopped paying the balance on once we split. So, I used his child support payments to supplement my income. He was going to pay me back with interest. That's why I haven't told Peter that Oliver is not his. He wouldn't have paid me anything had I told him the truth."

"I can't say that I have ever heard anything like this. 'Man Puts Woman In Debt.' 'Woman Makes Man Pay Back Debt By Collecting Child Support For A Child That Isn't His'," I say this as if I'm reading a headline. A few seconds go by and Silvie cracks up. We both start laughing. As messed up as it is, I understand her. She definitely knows how to think outside of the box.

"Well, when you say it like that, it does sound crazy." Silvie says laughing.

Her laugh makes my heart smile. I have a question for her.

"I'm trying to think about this logically. Wouldn't it have been easier to just make his biological father pay child support? Wouldn't that help you out with paying off of the debt? That way you could cut all ties with Peter. Oliver could spend time with his real dad and build a relationship with his flesh and blood."

"That sounds ideal, but Oliver's biological dad is worse than Peter. He was as mistake I made because I thought Peter was cheating. I cheated on Peter just so that I could be even. I thought that I'd feel better, but I didn't. I got drunk and didn't enforce that the man I cheated with protect himself. Despite his protests, I ended things with him. I had no idea that the child was his. When he found out that I broke up with Peter for good, he wanted to get back with me. He didn't want to accept that he was just someone I slept with to get back at my boyfriend. He hounded me to the point that it became scary. He stalked me. I tried to get an order of protection from him.

To get back at me, he served me with a court order to establish paternity of Oliver. He claimed that I was keeping him from his son. He said that he wasn't stalking me. It was a lie. This man was crazy. I reluctantly agreed to the test so that I could get an order of protection from him. Once I proved that Oliver was not his child, I could show the court that he's out of his mind. It all backfired when the test confirmed that he was Oliver's biological dad.

It was one of the worst days of my life. My stalker is my baby's father. He didn't want to be in Oliver's life. He didn't want to be a dad either. He wanted to have me. Once he finally got it through his head that there would never be an "us", he started using drugs more and disappeared for years. It wasn't until last year that I ran into him again. I was working at the shelter and he came in looking like life had a beef with him and won the fight."

The story Silvie was telling just kept getting harder and harder to listen to. It was like a Lifetime movie. She goes on about Oliver's dad.

"I acted as if I didn't know him every time he tried to get my attention or talk to me at the shelter. Like I said, he's crazy. I almost stopped volunteering at the shelter because of him. I told myself that I wasn't going to let him take my joy away. I get joy from helping at the shelter. I wasn't going to let him make me uncomfortable anymore.

For the most part, he got the hint and left me alone. Trying to engage with me was useless. Things were fine. At least I thought they were. Recently, he started fucking with me again. He'd say slick shit to me while in the cafeteria line. He'd eat his food and just stare at me. I could feel his gaze. It was like a horror movie scene. I could tell that he was using drugs. There was no telling what he'd do."

"So, your son's father goes to the same shelter I go to. That must mean I've seen him before. Who is he?"

"I'm sure that you've seen him before, but I don't think you know him."

"What's his name Silvie?"

"Elijah, you know his name. You read it on the paternity results."

"Oh, you're right? Tyson Brown. Well, I definitely don't know anyone by that name. Does he have a nickname? Maybe I'll recognize it."

"He wears a dirty white hat with a red bandana under it every day."

My mind flashed to that crackhead giving head to the man in the white cap with the red bandana. "Is Slick your son's father?"

"So, you do know him. Yes. Slick is his father and he's also the maniac that did this to me."

Silvie tells me what she remembers from the attack.

"I'd been holding my pee the entire ride home from the grocery store. When I entered my apartment, I remember thinking that it smelled like the shelter. I thought that was weird. I had no time to investigate the smell. I dropped all of my bags on the kitchen table and rushed to the bathroom. I usually put my groceries away as soon as I come in, especially the frozen foods. I couldn't hold my pee any longer. The frozen foods had to wait. The next thing I know, I'm on the toilet and Slick opens the bathroom door. I didn't lock the bathroom door because I was the only one at home.

There I am sitting on the toilet peeing and Slick comes in with his dick out. I'm shocked, terrified and embarrassed all at once. I try to get up from the toilet seat, but he pushes me back down. I remember his body odor. It took over the entire bathroom.

He calls someone else in. As soon as I saw her, relief washed over me. I recognized her from the shelter. I'd served this white girl food plenty of times. I'd always been nice to her; surely, she wasn't going to let Slick hurt me. Before passing out, I remember her drawing back her arm like she was going to hit me. That's it. That's all I remember. Honestly, I'm glad that's all that I can remember. I don't want to live my life reliving whatever they did to me." She pauses. "Wait. I do remember something else. I remember Slick asking me where his son was."

"Silvie, I can't lie. What they did to you has me wanting to commit homicide," I admit.

"Don't go doing that. How am I supposed to build a relationship with you if you get locked up? The only thing I'm worried about right now is if I was exposed to any diseases."

"Damn, I wasn't even thinking about that." I confess. Silvie sighs deeply.

"I've said a silent prayer that if I've been exposed to any diseases, I asked God to let them be the curable kind."

I close my eyes and silently pray for the same thing.

"Do you think that the police will catch him? I can't help but be pessimistic. A crime committed against a black women by a homeless black man. I can't see that being high on their priority list," she says while nervously trying to find something to do with her hands. She settles on rubbing them.

I take her hands in mine. I look her in her eyes and assure her that I won't rest until Slick is put in prison. Her hands feel cold. Silvie looks up at me with eyes that say "I hope so".

She did have a valid point though. I don't want to even delve into that, but I can't help but think about what she said. I rub her hands as we sit in silence. All the while, I'm thinking about the society we live in. Our society cares more about a white woman being assaulted than a black woman? What I know is that history has shown us that crimes against white women, suspected by black men are taken very seriously. It could cost a black man his life. Crimes against black women are minimized or overlooked. A motherfucking movement has to take place before society buys into the idea that they should be protected too. They deserve justice.

Society's response to black women being victimized has made black women not trust the system that has tried to tame them into a complacency and silence. Silvie breaks the silence.

"The detective told me that you found me. I don't know what led you to my apartment, but I thank you Elijah. Thank you for everything."

I've never felt rage hit me so quickly. It's heavy. The fight or flight feeling washes over me, except the feeling I'm experiencing is fight and fight. I can't sit here with

Silvie any longer. I have to go find Slick. I think about the words he said as I was getting into the cab.

"The pussy was better than I expected."

That's what he said. I thought he was talking about the chick that I saw him with. He wasn't referring to her. He was referring to Silvie. My heart is thumping like it's in a rush to go somewhere. I take a few deep breaths to slow my heart rate down but it's not working. I hate being tested. I always try my best to behave rationally, but I'm human. I'm not even close to being perfect. This will be where I fall short.

Slick has been testing me since the first time I crossed paths with him. Up until now, I've let him slide. I've been taught to ignore people that should know better, but act like they don't. I distance myself from those that I feel possess a negative energy. Today, I'm going to have to address things in a way that won't make my nana proud. I was taught that when I leave the house, the family leaves with me. That was a deterrent for me. I made good choices when I remembered that. Today, I leave my family at home.

Forgive me God. I'm going to fuck this nigga up!

Jean:

Imani's brown dreds are bouncing up and down right along with her full perky tits. She's expertly riding me. She's had to stop me from exploding two times now. She's been putting in work. I'm getting fucked instead of doing the fucking. She's in control. She smells so good and she feels even better. I can't take it. We've been fucking for at least thirty minutes. It doesn't look like she's even close to an orgasm. Her moaning sounds like she's humming. She's caught a rhythm. I try to sit up so that I can flip her over, but she isn't having it. She pushes my shoulders back down. Then she starts saying some of the dirtiest shit I've heard outside of Lil Kim's first album. It's over after that. I bust a nut and yell like I am officially pussy whipped.

She just stares at me. She's looking at me like she's waiting on my dick to re-inflate so that she can get her shit off. Once she sees I'm done, Imani gets off me and walks over to her pocketbook. She pulls out a vibrator from a small black case and walks back over to the bed. She lays beside me and says nothing. I hear the buzzing of the vibrator. She puts the vibrator on her pussy and gyrates. I can feel my dick getting hard all over again as I watch her. I guess I'm not done. I pull the covers off me so that she can see that I'm ready for another round. As soon as I get up to start round two, she lets out a deep moan of sheer satisfaction.

Now she's done. I attempt to get on top of her, but she pushes me off. As she heads to the bathroom to clean up, I feel insecure. I've never, to my knowledge, not pleased a woman. We may have used toys to get the party started, but a toy never had to shut down the party.

Imani comes out to the bathroom dressed as if she's ready to go.

"Jean, I have an early day tomorrow. I have to get back. I hope you understand."

Then she leaves. She doesn't even give me a chance to ask her to stay. She doesn't give me a chance to ask to see her again. What the fuck just happened here? How is she just going to leave a brother like that? What type of shit is this? Is this how black woman from Baltimore get down? Was she raised in a brothel? What type of woman treats sex like an everyday interaction instead of an intimate interaction? Was it that bad? If it was, she'd be the first to feel that way. I've put in a lot of work with a lot of different woman. Not once have I not satisfied a woman. Something must be wrong with her. It can't be me. I drift off to sleep second guessing myself.

**

Sunday wakes me up with more feelings of inadequacy. I dreamt that I had four-inch dick erect. No women wanted to get with me because they heard about how small my dick was. That wasn't a dream. That was a nightmare. I feel like I need a chance to redeem myself. I check my phone to see if Imani called or texted me. Nothing. This shit is really fucking with me. I did miss a text, but it wasn't from Imani. It was a picture of a voluptuous ass in a red lace thong. I didn't need to see the number to know who it was from. I'd know that ass anywhere. It was Sexy Suzie.

Wait a minute. Suzie lives in D.C. I'm not far from there. Maybe Sexy Suzie is interested in paying me a visit. I text her my location and ask if she'll be in the area anytime soon. She texts me back and said she's see me in two hours. That's all I needed to hear. Suzie arrived in ninety minutes. We both know what this visit's about. Suzie wastes no time. She plants her lips on me and it's on. I go to work on her.

I feel like I'm doing research. I'm paying special attention to what turns her on. I am watching how her body reacts to different things. I'm studying her every move. There's no doubt that she's enjoying herself. Then she does something that throws me off. She gets on top of me. Things were fine while I was in control. Now, she wants some control. Her tits are bigger than Imani's. They are barely bouncing up and down unlike like Imani's. I start to imagine that it is Imani on top of me. I forget all about Suzie. Then I give it to her with all my might. Imani climaxes… I mean Suzie climaxes and so do I.

Suzie doesn't immediately get up. She lays with me. She has her head on my chest. Suzie asks how long I'll be in the area. She'd like to see me again. I bet she does. She wants some more of this good dick. I tell her that I won't be here much longer, but if space and time permits I'll hit her up.

She looks up at me and smiles. Then she kisses me on my lips.

"Keeping your options open huh?" Suzie laughs as she gets out of the bed.

"Huh?" She catches me off guard with that remark.

"Anyway. If time and space permits hit me up."

That was it. She gets dressed in the bathroom and leaves the hotel room when she's done. When I get up to take a shower, I'm greeted by a stack of one. The bathroom floor is full of single dollar bills. The first time she left me a stipend it felt like gratuity. This time it felt disrespectful. She purposely left singles. The fact that they were on the floor wasn't a coincidence. She wanted me to have to bend down and pick them up like a stripper at the end of her set. Suzie got jokes I see. This is where the drama starts to show up with black women. They get some good dick and then start showing their ass. This will be the last time I see Suzie. I check my phone to see if Imani called. Nothing. Time for more research. I send a text to Randy. He agrees to meet me for coffee. I told him to wear sneakers because we'd be drinking coffee and walking the streets of Baltimore. I take my shower, get dressed and head out.

"Let's get this shit out of the way. I know you only called me up to get the 411 on my sister or else you would have invited the rest of the crew."

"Guilty." I say

"So, you really like her huh?" Randy asks.

"Man, it feels like she won't even let me like her. I can't even tell if she likes me."

"Well, I know my sister. If she isn't intrigued on some level, she wouldn't lay down with you. She told me that she was going to see you last night. So, I know y'all bumped uglies," he says laughing.

"Nothing about last night was ugly except for the way that she left," I say solemnly.

"What do you mean? I know you didn't disrespect my sister!" Ray says loud as fuck.

"No. Never that. I'm going to be honest with you. I don't think your sister was pleased with my performance."

"Oh so you couldn't hang?" Ray asks giggling in an octave usually attached to a female.

"I thought that I could hang. I thought I was doing a good job, but I finished first."

"Mmm, no bueno!" Ray confirms what I already knew.

"I know! She ended up getting her desired outcome with something battery operated. Then she up and bounced. She straight left yo." I'm almost whining.

"Well you can do two things. If you are really interested in her, chase her. Your other option is to call it a loss and know that the next time you step to a woman of her caliber you better come correct. No pun intended." Randy cracks up at his play with words.

"You are right. Nothing worth having comes easy." We both crack up at my unintentional pun.

Randy tells me that he texted the guys and they are going to meet us at the mall to do some shopping. Jerome needs some support as he does takes part in some retail therapy. We spend the day shopping. I find a gift store a block before the mall. I buy something there for Imani. It was time to come correct.

8

RECONSTRUCTION ERRORS

Shawn:

In the past, being in a room with complete silence was comforting. Nowadays, silence scares me. Myself and my outside self-conversations have become louder. It's like they wait for there to be silence to start acting up. It's hard to rest with all the chatter. This morning something different happened. Who I identify as my outside self, had a different voice. It was a woman's voice.

When I first heard the voice, I thought someone was in the room with me. I actually walked around my house looking inside of my closets expecting to find someone hiding. No such luck. It was only me in the house. It spooked me. I tried to convince myself that I didn't hear a woman's voice. I told myself that maybe it was someone outside. Maybe it was my Alexa device. The only problem with that is the voice sounded as if they were standing behind me speaking into my ear. I turn on the music to rid myself of the silence and hopefully rid myself of the unwelcomed guest.

The music motivates me to go to the gym. I don't want to work out alone. I text Elijah from the gym. I ask if he wants to meet me at Planet Fitness. I could really use an encouraging gym partner. He texts me back and says that he's busy today. Maybe we can work out tomorrow. I text him back saying that sounds like a plan. I decide to stay home and drink some beers while I watch ESPN.

***

I wake up and it's dark. It was daylight when I was watching television. I don't know what time it is, but It has to be late because it is dark as hell in my living room. The television is the only thing illuminating the room. I get up to turn on the light and I hear someone.

"Where the fuck are you going? Lay your fat ass back down. Nobody wants you. Nobody likes you. They just use you. You've said it yourself. Everyone takes from you. Donna took your virginity. Her brother took your 'virgin' fiancée. You let that family do a number on you. Didn't' you? When are you going to stand up for yourself? When are you going to stop letting all of these people take from you?

Maybe she was right, maybe you don't like pussy because you are a pussy. Is that it? I know you heard that the kids in school called you a faggot back in the day. You've been dressing like a gay dude since your momma let you start dressing yourself. Embrace it. You're gay. Admit it. You ain't really mad that Nakia cheated. You're mad because you love the man she cheated on you with. What I want to know is are you a top or a bottom? You seem like a bottom to me."

"SHUT UP!" I scream. And just like that the voice stopped.

I upgrade my beer to Hennessey. I need a real drink. My head hurts. I'm getting one of those headaches again. I pop a few Tylenol and wash it down with the brown liquor. I have to go to work tomorrow. I shouldn't be drinking like this, but I don't care at this point. I text my mother and tell her that the headaches have started again. She calls me right away.

"Hi, Ma." I'm hoping she can't detect that I'm emotional. I want to cry.

"Hi, Son. I'm worried about you… Shawn you may need to see a physician about those headaches if they are back. How often are you experiencing them? I knew that you should have seen a physician when you started having them in high school. That's my fault for not forcing you to go get checked out when you were younger. Now that they are back, you need to go. If something is wrong, you need to find out now rather than later. You stopped complaining of headaches right when you graduated. I never thought any more of it. Make an appointment in the morning Shawn."

***

Morning got here quick. I'm moving in slow motion. I can't seem to pull it together. I'm sure the Hennessey is why I'm having such a hard time. I'm in a funk. I don't feel like going to work. I need to take a sick day, but I have too many things that I need to finish up at work. There are a few departments waiting on my data report that I promised to have to them today. I'm grateful that I ironed my stuff off for work for the next few days before I went to bed on Friday night. I pull an outfit out of my closet and try my best to get it together.

I press my remote car starter and pack a few pieces of fruit and a few bottles of water to take with me to work. Today, I will stop putting things off. I will start eating right. I'm going to give up alcohol until I get my weight down. I'm going to stop eating junk food. I'm going to commit to the gym at least three times a week. Most importantly, I'm going to call my primary care to get an appointment to address these headaches. I may need to see a neurologist. I also decide to forgive Peter and Nakia for their bullshit.

I am falling apart. My work life is fine but my personal life is a mess. I need to get back to me. I need to make myself a priority and stop taking care of everyone else before myself. If I'm going to forgive Peter and Nakia, I have to forgive Donna too. If I don't, I'll drive myself crazy. I already feel like I am halfway there. I know once the headaches go away, the voices will too. They did last time.

I walk out my back door and see Nakia standing by my car. I think that I must be seeing things just like I've been hearing things lately. She is standing beside my car with a can of paint.

"Just so you know I'm on Facebook live. So, don't even think about trying to come after me. I will have my people fuck you up. I've included my location on this post too," she says as if she feels protected.

"Why are you here, Nakia?"

"I'm here because I've been doing some digging of my own. And since you like to put other people's business out there, I think it's only fair that your business be put out there too," she says while turning the phone to her face so that Facebook world can see her face.

"What are you talking about? I don't have time for this. Leave my yard. I gotta get to work."

"If you take one more step, this bucket of paint is going to be splattered all over your car Shawn." Nakia is on the passenger side of the car holding her paint can. I call her bluff and keep walking to my car. My car senses that my key is nearby and unlocks as soon as I get close to it. I open the door and I feel something wet dripping down the back of my head, neck, back and legs. *Did she really just splash paint on me?*

"She sure did. HA! Not only did she splash paint on you, but she got the right color too." The familiar female voice chimes in. I try to block out the voice. My phone alerts me that I have notifications from Facebook. The alerts seem to be coming in one after another. I turn around and look at Nakia. She's standing there with an empty bucket breast cancer awareness pink paint in one hand and her IPhone still streaming live in the other. My notification alerts keep coming. The constant beeps are irritating me. Nakia looks at me as if she is daring me to do step to her. Then she starts.

"Now that I have your attention. Like I was saying, since you like digging up people's past, I did some digging of my own. I must admit. I was shocked and relieved when I found this out. You've got at least one skeleton in your closet. Yup and I'm so glad I get to share this with the world. You should thank me because after today, you'll be able to live your life as your true self." The female voice interrupts before I can respond to Nakia.

"This chick is hilarious! You were going to marry her? She's pretty, and she's a drama queen. There's wasn't enough room for two queens anyway." I scream at the voice.

"Shut up!" I yell again. Nakia thinks I'm speaking to her and responds.

"No, I won't shut up. You had this coming. Maybe you'll think twice before you put folk's private information out there next time. You don't know how many lives you affected. And to think, you had some dirt too." The female voice chimes in again.

"I can't wait to hear this. What does she have on you Shawn? What did she dig up?"

"I don't know." I tell the female voice. I just want to get out of here. I can't take this. I want to drive off, but I don't want to mess up my car with all this pink paint on me. Nakia is blocking my path to my back-door step. I try to get by her but she is making it difficult. I ask her to leave again and to get out of the way.

"Facebook! Do you see this? Better yet, do you hear this? He wants me to leave. Well, let me tell you why he wants me to leave. Go ahead back in your house. It doesn't matter at this point. I'm going to tell the world your secret whether you are standing here or not." The female voice won't leave me alone.

"Oh, I'm sticking around for this. You got any popcorn in the house Shawn?"

"Ok Facebook make sure you share this on your page once I'm done. And I'm just about done."

I open my screen door and then I hear Nakia telling Facebook why she chose pink paint. She told the world that I've been on the down low. She said I prefer men. She said I've been living a lie. I've been lying to everyone including her. To think that she was going to marry a gay man disgusts her. While she's' saying this, the female voice is yelling in my ear.

"This chick should have her own show! Did you hear her tell everyone that you've been on the Down Low? She basically told folks you've been fronting and been doing men in secrecy. It's not going to matter to them that it was only one time. Men don't have the luxury of experimenting. Men can't be bi-sexual. Once you enter another man or allow him to enter you, you're gay. That's it. I'd say be a man about it and own up to it, but you and I already had this conversation. You don't like pussy because you are a pussy. Here's another person fucking with you and you're doing nothing about it. You didn't even have the opportunity to come out of the closet on your own terms. Nakia took that from you, another person taking from you. Did you hear her? She just said that someone named Donna Jones confirmed this information. I heard she was a drug addict. I don't know how credible she is, but I guess Nakia didn't care. Uh Oh! There it is. She gave a name. I must say, I'm surprised at the name Shawn. When did this happen?" Nakia repeats the name in a slow and exaggerated way. while looking at her phone and talking to her live Facebook audience.

"Donna Jones said that Shawn Carson got fucked by her brother Peter. I hope Peter sees this. If anyone is his Facebook friend please tag him for me. Donna said that she found Peter and Shawn in her brother's room doing things that a man and a woman usually do to each other. This happened when they were in Junior High. They thought that she was napping, but she wasn't. In case anyone is wondering, Donna confirmed that Shawn is a bottom y'all. We never had sex, so I wouldn't know." Nakia says laughing obnoxiously into her phone.

Then it happened. The female voice became my own. She took over my mind and my actions. I became her. She became me.

Elijah:

It's Monday and I have a lot to do. First things first, I head to Silvie's house to drop off her car. Then I get an Uber from her house to Woburn to get to the lottery office to cash in my ticket and collect my check. Next, I take the Uber to Eastern Bank. I needed to make sure that I took care of that deposit before I take my field trip to Boston to fuck up Slick. I'm dressed in my boots, jeans and a hoodie. When I finish up at the bank, I ask the same Uber driver to take me to Boston. He is a brother. I told him that I needed to make a few stops. He said he was cool with that. I paid him up front and separately for each trip.

The Uber driver's name is Jeff. He is telling me about a concert that he went to at the Berklee Performance Center. He asks if I ever heard of two brothers called Black Violin. I tell him that I haven't. He tells me that I have to check them out on YouTube. They play the violin but with flavor. According to him they are two very talented brothers. He starts talking to me about stereotypes. Black Violin looks like two regular brothers from around the way. You'd never guess that they play the violin. I didn't grow up seeing any brothers play the violin. They are not the stereotype. If we keep it real, most brothers aren't the stereotype. The stereotype is what the media perpetuates with their targeted news reporting. The stereotype is the minority, not the majority. Yet, folks get caught up in believing the hype and assimilating to it. The black man is feared because of the stereotypes placed upon us. America has internalized the stereotypes to the point that they equate black men with crime and violence.

Here we are having this conversation and I'm about to feed right into the stereotype. Jeff discloses how he got down in his youth. He said he was the stereotypical black kid from the projects. He didn't see himself making it out of his neighborhood. He sold drugs. He stole from people. He didn't finish school. He had no long-term goals. No daddy in the home, you know all the makings of a man destined to perpetuate the stereotype of being jail-bound.

Then his mom sent him to live with a cousin down south, fearing that he'd kill himself or get killed. It was there that he met a woman in the neighborhood that took an interest in him and steered him on the right path. She encouraged him to go back to high school. He even went on to college and finished. Jeff's driving Uber to make some extra money to send his mother on a cruise. She's always wanted to go, but never had enough money to go and pay the bills. I don't want to expose this brother to any of the shit that I'm about to start. I'm honest with him and tell him that he can drop me off because my next stop is to beat somebody's ass.

He tells me that he's good. He said that I seem like a reasonable brother. If I'm taking an Uber specifically to beat someone's ass, he must deserve it. He'll be here waiting when I'm done as long as I don't kill the dude. He's out if that happens. I'm in front of the shelter and I don't see Slick hanging around. I ask Jeff to drive me to the intersection of Mass Ave and Melnea Cass. He's usually out there at the light begging for money. Jeff tells me to be smart about things.

"What exactly are you beating this dudes ass for?" Jeff asks.

"He raped someone that I love."

"Nuff said. I needed to see what type of handling he needed before I make this call."

"Make what call?" I ask.

"Just sit tight. Let's first ride down there to see if he's out there. Once we know for sure, I got you.

"I don't want to involve you in this Jeff, thanks for the offer though."

"I said I got you. Sit tight. Is that dude with the white cap and red bandana?"

"Yah, that's that nigga." I say heatedly.

"Ok, let's go make a stop to Mission Hill real quick."

"Ok man, whatever, I just need this nigga to pay."

"I'm going to bring you to the shelter you said you know him from. Go there and make sure that your seen. Get something to eat or whatever folks do when they go there," He says laughing. I don't know why, but I trust him.

"Alright, I take it I'll hear from you soon."

"You know it." And then he's gone.

I don't get a call until an hour later. He tells me to meet him at the bus stop near the shelter. When he arrives, he tells me that he has a gift for me. We drive to his homie's place in Mission Hill.

"Oh, So you had these big mother fuckers kidnap me?" Slick yells when he sees me.

I look at Jeff and the two brothers that have him tied to a chair. Jeff looks at me.

"You want a fair fight or you want to treat him the way he treated your lady?"

"We made him tell us what he did to your girl. I'm sorry man. He's a sick bastard."

"Yah, untie that nigga."

As soon as he's untied he stands up and smiles, then he smells his fingers. That was it. I blacked out on that nigger. He didn't have a chance. I beat him down like he deserved and a little more for all the times he fucked with me in the streets. When I was done, my hands were swollen and all his teeth were gone. He'll be an ideal bitch for the niggas in prison with all gums and no teeth. I went to punch him again, but Jeff stopped me.

"Chill homie, unless you want to kill him. That's what's gonna happen if you hit him anymore. Besides, we recorded him admitting to raping Silvie. This nigga's going to jail. He's going to turn himself in right after we drop his ass off at the police station."

"He can't go to the police station like that. They'll ask what happened to him."

"We got that covered. Did it look like this is the first time we did something like his to a motherfucker? Don't worry. We got you. Slick's gonna tell the police that he got into a fight with another one of his homeless brethren. The police ain't going to waste time investigating an assault on a homeless dude by another homeless dude."

He has a point. Jeff has no idea how right he is. He doesn't know that last week I was sleeping out on the streets just like Slick. I just met this man and he had my back like we've been boys for years.

"You're gonna have to take the bus or train to wherever your next stop is. I'm off the clock. I'll hit you up tomorrow E."

When did I become E? Thanks, Jeff. You're good people."

"No doubt," he says and I give the other two gentleman dap as I leave to walk to the Orange Line. I'm walking down Tremont St. thinking about the last few days. My hands hurt. I stop and grab a water from my backpack. There are only a few Ibuprofen left. I take two. My hands are throbbing. I peel off the work gloves that I wore to fuck Slick up. Underneath I have on two pairs of plastic gloves. I wore two just in case one pair broke from the blows I was planning on inflicting. My headphones make it to my ears instinctively. As I wait for the Oak Grove train, I listen to "Gonna Be Alright" by Mali Music." I zone out and think about life as I sing his lyrics.

Peter:

I thought I was going to be able to hand him a bowl of cereal for breakfast. This little dude says he wants eggs and toast. So, here I am frying him some eggs and Crystal walks in.

"I'm home!" She says all happy and shit.

I don't respond. I continue frying Oliver's eggs and act like she's not here. Oliver doesn't get the memo. He greets Crystal.

"Hi, I'm Oliver," he says all friendly and shit.

"Oh, I didn't know you had a guest Peter."

"I'm no guest. I'm Oliver," he says matter-of-factly.

"Well, Hello Oliver. I'm Crystal," she says.

"Nice to meet you," Oliver replies.

I'm impressed with this little dude's manners. I guess Silvie is doing something right. Crystal's dumb self comes over to me while I'm cooking and slaps my ass. She's tripping. She sees my son's here. Why would she do some stupid shit like that? Oliver chimes in before I can tell her to fuck off

"My mom told me that it is not ok to hit someone. You'll get in trouble."

I like this kid.

"Oh I'm sorry Oliver. I was just playing with your dad. It won't happen again."

"As long as you've learned your lesson…" Oliver says as I snicker.

I serve Oliver his breakfast and tell him to sit at the table and watch television. I head into the bedroom to talk to Crystal.

"Where the fuck you been Crystal?"

"I was out. What do you care?"

"Out where? Is your phone broken? You see I called and texted you."

"Oh, Did you miss me Peter?"

"Listen your bugging. You know you're wrong for that shit. I pay for you to have a nice day and you disrespect me and make me regret doing something nice for you." I complain.

"Disrespect you? You regret doing something nice for me? Nigger please!" She says with too much comfort.

Up until this point, I've never heard Crystal use the word nigger. She said it with such ease that I figure she's used it before. I'm ready to slap the shit out of her. I can't because my son is in the kitchen. The last thing I need is for him to go back telling his mom that he saw me hit a nice white lady. She'll never let me see him again. I also don't need to get arrested for assaulting a white woman. If they don't kill a black man for hurting a white woman, they lock him up and throw away the key. This white bitch ain't worth it. She sees that my son is here and is taking this opportunity to act brand new because she knows I won't do anything with him here. Then she throws something small at me.

"I found that earring in your car. Why would someone's earring fall off in your car? Who did you have in your car and what were you two doing that led to it falling off? Huh?"

I say nothing.

"That's what I fucking thought," she yells.

"Crystal lower your voice. You see my son is in the next room."

"I don't give a shit about him or you. My brother warned me that a nigger couldn't do anything for me outside of the bedroom. You know something, he was right! You know what else? Take your gorilla ass and your little H&M monkey baby out of my house! Right now, before I call the police. You think you can cheat on me and get away with it. Fuck you and whatever nigger cunt you're sleeping with."

It took every fiber of restraint that I had in me not to punch this bitch in the face. Instead, I grabbed my essentials, a few clothes and my son and left. I said nothing to her. She kept talking shit the entire time I was packing. The only thing she didn't do was put her hands on me. I can't say that I would have left without at least shaking the shit out her if she did that. My phone rings as I'm putting Oliver into my car. It's a number that I don't recognize and I don't pick up numbers that aren't already stored in my phone. I let it go to voice mail. Then I listen to it.

"This message is for Peter Jones. This is Kathleen. I'm a nurse at Mass General Hospital. You are listed as one of the emergency contacts for Silvie Vick. If this information is still current, please contact me at …"

The voice message is cut off by multiple Facebook alerts. I'll check them later. Right now, I need to get to Mass

General and see what's up with Silvie. I tried calling the nurse back, but she was with a patient. I was too impatient to wait for her call. Oliver and I ride over to MGH to check on his mom. Man, I hope she's ok.

Jean:

Imani must have felt sorry for me, because ten text messages later she's agreed to meet me at my hotel for dinner. I get a call from a number that I don't recognize. I'm getting ready to meet Imani downstairs for dinner. Whoever it is can wait. I change my mind and look at the number to see if it is my sister. It's not. I don't recognize the number. I let it go to voice mail.

I take one last look in the mirror at myself. My nose hairs are clipped. My nails are cut low and filed. My line-up is fresh. Randy put me on to a barber in the area that cuts his hair. I will admit he's nice with the clippers. I'm not a hairy dude, but I shaved the hair off my chest and made sure I didn't miss any pubic hairs. I learned that the ladies are more willing to give head when your shit looks groomed. I also realized that your dick looks bigger and better when you shave.

I grab the gift that I bought for Imani and head to the elevators. My room is on the top floor. The elevator stops at the next floor and a group of young women get on the elevator. The elevator is packed. They are all dressed as if they are going to the club. Under normal circumstances, I would have taken this opportunity to compliment them and find out where they are heading to. Not tonight. My focus is on Imani. Don't get me wrong, a few of these ladies are extra sexy. I almost tempted to see what's up with them just in case things don't work out with Imani tonight. I don't though. I keep my eyes on the prize.

"Mmm you smell good," one of the girls says.

I just smile. I don't say anything.

"You look just like that man Ralph Angel from Queen Sugar. Anyone ever tell you that?"

"No," I say as I look to see what floor we are. Five more stops until the lobby.

"Well you do, but you're finer than him. I didn't think that was possible until I saw you boo."

She tries to hold my hand. I put my hands in my pocket. I know her number is coming soon. Two more stops. She opens my jacket and slips a business card in my inside pocket of my suit jacket. She licks her lips and instructs me to call her. As soon as we get out of the elevator, I take the card out of my pocket and throw it away, not without taking a picture of it. It says that she does hair braiding and weaving. Hey, you never know. I might need her services.

I take my seat at the table and wait for Imani to arrive. She's late, but I don't care. As long as she shows up, I have a chance. One minute later, in comes Imani. I can feel her before I even look up to see her. She has on a short jean shirt dress. She has on brown thigh high boots. They are so close to the color of her skin that it almost looks like she's bare. An African print necklace made of what looks like three rings with green, brown and yellow material wrapped around it hangs down on her chest. On her ears are drop earrings made of wood. I attempt to get up and pull out her seat, but she insists that I sit. There she goes positioning herself again. She likes to be in control on more levels than in the bedroom. When she sits down I can see that her earrings have the word "yes" carved into them. Hopefully, that's what she'll be saying in my bed tonight.

"Thank you for coming, " I say to her genuinely.

"My brother told me that you were crying. I figured I had to at least check on you," she laughs.

"I'm sure he did," I say laughing right with her.

"What's up? You couldn't find anyone to keep you company tonight?"

"I wanted to see you. I am not worried about anyone else."

"Is that so? We just met. Are you that sprung already?" She asks confidently.

"I'm sure there is the potential for me to be sprung, but you won't even give me a chance to tell you that I'm feeling you. Why is that? Why'd you run out of the hotel room so soon last night?" I ask.

"Because it was time to go," she says nothing more.

"I was hoping you'd give me another chance and allow me to learn you."

"You mean get to know me," she's quick to correct me.

"No. I meant what I said. I want to learn you. That's deeper than getting to know you."

"Last night I didn't take the time to learn you. I took for granted that my big ole dick would be enough to please you. I'm sorry that you didn't enjoy yourself."

I feel like she is looking through me. She says nothing. She just stares at me. I meet her gaze to let her know that I'm the man sitting at this table, not her. She smiles, but still says nothing.

"I bought something for you." I say. I don't wait for her to respond. I reach down in the bag that I had sitting on the floor under the table. I hand her the beautifully gift-wrapped box.

"Please except my apology. Allow me the opportunity to learn you Imani."

She unwraps the gift and opens it slowly. It was like she was scared to open it. When she finally opens it; she grins.

"You're learning."

I smile back at her.

"Any woman that carries her own gadgets with her is a woman that requires a man to take time to discover her. I'm confident enough to promise you that I'll keep trying until I get it right. If a toy is what it takes there, I'll be the one using the toy on you. They'll be no more of you finishing with your pocketbook penetrator. Whether it takes my dick or this super-duper guaranteed to make you quiver vibrator, I'll be facilitating your future orgasms. Are you ok with this Imani? Can I learn you? Can we spend some time exploring your likes and dislikes with the goal of adding me to your likes?

"I like that you put yourself out there and made yourself vulnerable. Only strong men can do that comfortably. What I don't like is that you think that you can make your language flowery and think that I won't pick up on game."

"I'm confused Imani. What game do you think that I am trying to run on you?"

"Jean, it sounds like you asked me to be your fuck buddy. You ain't fooling nobody. You can disguise it any way that you want, but what it comes down to is you and I fucking. Is that what you want me for Jean? Do you just want to fuck me to the point of climax to repair your ego, because that's what it sounds like?" She asks with a hint of attitude.

"Yup. You're right. I do want to fuck you to the point of a climax and then do it again and again and again. Yes, my ego took a hit last night, but that's not why I want you.

It wasn't by accident that we met. The way I see it, I'm going to be the man to make your strong ass submit. Don't get it twisted. I'm not going to do it with my dick. I'm going to do it with my willingness to also submit to you. The vibe that you're giving off feels like it's been a while since anybody has made you fall in love. That changes with me. I'm going to make it impossible not to love me," I say this with true sincerity. She's who I've been searching for.

"I give you some pussy one time and you're already trying to have papers on me. Let's not get ahead of ourselves. Love is a word that I don't toss around lightly. Let's see how mechanically inclined you are after dinner and then take it from there."

I hear her say "papers on me" and I think about how many times I've complained about that same thing. I laugh to myself. Then I ask, "Mechanically inclined?"

"Yes. Mechanically Inclined. Let's see what you can do with this super-duper guaranteed to make you quiver vibrator," she laughs. I laugh with her. *I've found my queen.*

We order dinner and she asks me something that I wasn't expect to talk about during this date. I was thinking we'd talk about everything from pop culture to politics. This woman wants to talk about matters of the heart.

"So... Jean, who broke your heart?"

"What makes you think that someone broke my heart?" I ask.

"If you haven't had your heart broken yet, how can you truly appreciate your next relationship? Broken hearts are blessings in disguise. They teach you about love and how to handle love."

The waitress brings our drinks to the table. She mixes up the order and gives Imani my drink. As I'm about to correct her, Imani hands the drink to me. The waitress apologizes.

"Back to your heart-who broke it?" She's staring at me.

"Why don't you tell me who broke your heart first?" I feel like a coward.

"Seriously? Is this how you handle difficult conversations? What are you afraid of?"

"Nothing. I'm not afraid of anything. I just thought it was kind of early to be revealing my relationship skeletons." I feel myself sweating a little. Then I tell her.

"My ex-girlfriend Claire told me that she was pregnant with my baby. She lied. It was her light skinned ex-boyfriend's baby. I loved her. I thought she loved me. It wasn't until I met her mother that I found out that Claire and I were just fucking. We weren't in a relationship." Imani interrupts with a question.

"Why did you mention that her ex-boyfriend is light skin?"

"Oh, there's relevance. I mentioned his lack of melanin because Claire's mother only allowed her to date dudes that resemble Common. Her ex actually looked like Common— had the same swag and everything. Anyway, long story short, Claire and her mom were arguing about some family shit. I was in Claire's bedroom because I spent the night. My clothes were in the front room so he mom knew I was in the house. That didn't stop her from putting all of Claire's business out there making sure she was loud enough for me to hear. That's when I found out that Common was the real father-to-be."

Imani laughs.

"I'm sorry! It's not funny-but you called him Common." She's still laughing.

"I guess it is kind of funny thinking about it now. I'm a fan of Common. I had to stop listening to him and watching him in movies because of this shit." I say laughing with her.

We eat our meal and talk about something lighter. We decide to address that it is probably to address one traumatic event per date. Just as the waiter leaves the bill at the table, my phone rings. It's that same number. Imani notices that I am ignoring the phone and tells me to answer it.

"Hello...."

A few minutes later, I hang up the phone and Imani can tell that I'm not ok. One minute, I'm having the time of my life. The next minute I'm filled with rage. I tell Imani that I'm going to have to cut the night short. There's a family matter that I must deal with. I tell her that I will be booking a flight back to Boston tonight. My emotions are all over the place. I have to get home to Silvie and Oliver.

I walk Imani out. I honestly couldn't tell you what she or I said. I do remember giving her a peck on the lips. That's about it. I was in a state of disbelief. Who would do this to Silvie? And why the fuck didn't the hospital call me. Silvie's been in the hospital for twenty-four hours and nobody contacted me. I know I'm her emergency contact. Why the fuck was Peter the one to call me? I know that Silvie and I had a pretty bad argument, but why didn't she call me? At the end of the day, we are each other's immediate family. That fact doesn't change because we had an argument. Family is supposed to be there no matter what. I hate that she didn't feel she could call me.

***

I don't know how I made it back to Boston, It's all a blur. What I do know is that I'm not going home. I'm going straight to MGH to check on my sister and my nephew. Peter texted me the building and the floor Silvie's on. I get an eerie feeling when I enter the hospital. I hate hospitals. They are so depressing. There's nothing but sickness and death in these places. I put my feelings aside and head to the elevators.

I make it up to the ninth floor. I push the handicap button with my elbow so that the door opens automatically. I'm not trying to touch anything in this place. I look for the hand sanitizer dispenser that I know that have on each floor of hospitals, at least they are supposed to. I see one on the wall. I walk over to it before going to the desk to ask which room Silvie is in. I hear my name.

"Yo Jean! Over here yo!" Peter yells.

"Uncle JEAN!" Oliver yells and runs over to me.

"Mommy is sick. She's in the hospital. My daddy said she will be better soon, but she can't come home yet. Am I going to stay here with Mommy?"

Peter answers, "No son. You're going to stay with daddy until your mom gets better."

"But you don't have a home daddy. The white lady that hit you said you have to get out. She said that she didn't want you to come back. She said to take your H&M monkey with you. Remember daddy? Is an H&M monkey different than the monkeys you take me to see at the Franklin Park Zoo?" Oliver asks innocently.

Really niggah? Shaking my head, I tell Oliver that he's going to stay with me because his Dad has to work. Peter doesn't fight me on this. I look at him like the piece of shit that he is and dare him to disagree. Judging from what my nephew just revealed, this nigger had my nephew around some bullshit. Why am I not surprised?

"They told us to wait out here because she's being examined again. They will call us to come in when they are done."

232

I sit down across from Peter. I give Oliver my iPhone and headphones so that he can play a game and I can have a grown folks conversation with Peter. I don't need to give him any instructions. This kid knows how to work the phone better than I do.

"So, what do you know?"

"I didn't get much information. When we got here, they were ready to examine her and kicked us out. All I know is that she was raped and that she hit her head."

"Do they know who did it?" I ask as anger starts to consume me again.

"I don't know." Peter says.

"Niggah what do you know!" I say loud enough that Oliver looks up.

The white woman at the reception desk looks up too. I check myself. I'm the last person that wants to give a white woman a reason to put me into the "threatening black man box". I make it a daily priority to show people that I am not the stereotype.

I size her up quickly. I'd bet money that she's sized me up too. She assumes I'm not college educated. I live in the ghetto. I have at least three kids with three different women, who I refer to as my bitch, baby mama or that hoe. She thinks that I sell drugs. If not that, she thinks I'm a thief. I've had to have been to jail at least once because black men aren't individuals; they are the stereotype.

Peter looks at me like I'm lucky his son is here. I didn't realize that I stood up when I raised my voice. I slowly take my seat and try to calm myself down enough not to scare the white folks. I apologize to Peter. He says nothing. He just sits there looking at the door. He's waiting on the medical staff to come out and let us know that we can go in. I sit in silence with him. Oliver is in his own world although I wish I could be in that world with him. This world chews you up and spits you back out.

A nurse comes out and tells us that we can see Silvie now. Silvie looks surprised to see me as I enter her room. I don't know what I was expecting to see, but she looked better than expected. She puts her arms out so that she can get a hug from Oliver. Once she's done hugging and kissing him, she sends him to sit on the vacant bed divided by the curtain. He continues to play games on my phone with the headphones on.

"I know that you both want to know what happened. After I tell you everything, there is something else that I want to talk to you about. It concerns Oliver."

"If you're going to tell me that he needs me to be more present in his life, no need. I get it. I'm going to try my best to be there more for my little homie."

"Let's hope you have the same attitude once we talk."

Silvie tells us the horrific story, at least all that she can remember. I have tears in my eyes when she's done. Peter is pacing the floor. Oliver dozed off to sleep on the other hospital bed. Silvie asks that I take Oliver home with me when we finish talking.

"No problem. He can stay with me for as long as you need." I say.

"What did you want to talk about us about?" Peter asks.

What Silvie tells us sounds like the behavior of one of those black chicks on a reality show I often refer to. I'm now pacing back and forth. We are both trying to process the information. Peter has tears in his eyes. He's staring at the paternity results. Then he looks at the Bible. Out of nowhere he yells.

"You Bitch! You knew that he wasn't my son and still continued to take money from me!"

"You better sit your ass down and take the word Bitch out your mouth when referring to my sister Nigger... unless you want us both to go to jail tonight," I say as I stand up. My sister may be wrong, but he's not going to disrespect her. Peter stands there as if he doesn't know what to do.

"Before I catch a case for fucking both of you up, I'm leaving." Peter says.

"Wise choice," I say.

Peter gets to the door and says "It looks like you got what you deserved Silvie. Lose my motherfucking number."

I really should have jumped on that nigger for saying what he said, but I understand his pain. Shit like this happens more often than you think. It happened to me. That's probably why Silvie felt like she couldn't tell me.

Silvie knew how much I was hurt by that experience. I stopped trying to be in relationships with light-skinned women, because so many of them have been diseased by colorism. The dark-skinned women have low self-esteem because of it. The light-skinned women think they are superior because of it. Neither one of them would probably admit to it, but I know it exists. I truly believe that it will be easier to build the self-esteem of a dark-skinned woman than try to humble a light-skinned woman. The truth is that our shit is complicated. There are so many outside factors that affect how we interact with each other, never mind the shit that's exclusive to our ethnic group.

Silvie and I just sit in silence. I can tell that she is emotionally overwhelmed. I don't ask any questions. She sits and reads the Bible. After about ten minutes, Silvie tells me to leave. It's late. Oliver is still sleeping. I wake him up so that he can tell his mother goodnight. Silvie hugs him like she never wants to let him go. She'll be going home within the next few days. She asks if it would be ok for Oliver to stay with me until she figures some things out. She doesn't want him at the apartment. She didn't want to be there either, but she needed some time to herself to decompress. I tell her to take all the time that she needs. Oliver will be fine. We leave just as I'm getting a text. It's from Imani.

Hope everything is ok. If It isn't. Let me know how I can help.

I get home and put Oliver to sleep in my spare bedroom. I might as well call it his bedroom because nobody else ever sleeps in there besides him. Once he's settled, I text Imani. She texts me back that she's still up. If I want to talk instead of texting, feel free to call her. I call her. I tell her what happened to my sister. I tell her what's happened in my past relationships. I tell her my flaws. I make myself vulnerable.

I'm not surprised that I haven't been able to find a queen. I'm surprised that I think I finally found her. It's still early, but I'm excited about the possibilities. Imani has this regal energy about her. Imani embraces her brown skin. She's unapologetically black. She's strong. She's independent. She's smart with an opinion. She keeps it real. She's got sex appeal. She's funny. Imani is my Michelle Obama

We talk until the next morning. I haven't done anything like that since high school. We even FaceTime each other while she tested out the gift I bought her. Let's just say that not only is there a quiver feature, but there's also a squirt feature. I am flying her out to Boston next weekend so that we can test them out in person.

Elijah:

As I'm listening to Mali Music, I run across and article on social media. ECCO is fighting for a Criminal Justice reform bill in Massachusetts. They want Governor Charlie Baker to sign a bill into law that does a number of things. According to Rabbi Margie, there is a sixty percent recidivism rate in Massachusetts. It costs the state forty-nine thousand dollars per person a year when you send someone to jail.

Rabbi Margie said that she's not saying that Massachusetts should be easy on crime. Massachusetts needs to be smart about crime. We need to prevent the number of people going to jail for the wrong reason. We need to help people coming out of jail make good choices so that they don't end up back in jail. She mentioned that Kentucky, which is not a liberal state, has proven that when you make changes you get results. The number of people in jail and the rate of crime has reduced.

Black people are eight times more likely to end up in jail than white people. Latinos are five times more likely to end up in jail than white people. The bill that she's fighting for reforms the bail system. It gets rid of some of the mandatory sentencing low level drug offenses. It raises the age that kids can go to juvenile detention. I didn't know that you could go to Juvi at age seven in Massachusetts. That's first grade. That sounds crazy to me. We don't know the law until we are affected by it. I'm going to have to follow Rabbi Margie on Twitter.

I search through Spotify for a neo-soul compilation. As I am searching, a call interrupts me. I recognize the number and immediately have anxiety. Why would they be calling me so late? I hold my breath when I answer the call.

"Hello, Am I speaking to Mr. Elijah Joseph?"

"Yes. This is he."

"Mr. Joseph, my name is … you're listed as healthcare proxy and next of kin… stroke."

The connection reception on the Orange line is choppy. I couldn't hear everything that the nursing home said, but heard enough. I get off at the next stop and call an Uber to my Nana's nursing home in Lynn. I don't know if she's dead or alive, but a stroke isn't good.

I call the nursing home back and explain that I got a call regarding Mrs. Joseph but my line got disconnected because I was on the train. She connects me to whoever I was speaking to before. I'm told that my grandmother isn't at the nursing home. She is already on an ambulance to Mass General Hospital. I cancel my Uber. I get back on the train and head to Mass General.

I shut my eyes and start to silently pray. *Please don't take my grandmother from me Lord. Restore her health. Increase her quality of life. I need her. I haven't had a chance to tell her about everything that's happened. I have a new job. I hit the lottery. I'm in love. We haven't gotten a chance to celebrate. I used a penny to scratch it off like she told me. Lord, please don't punish me for hurting Slick. I didn't kill him. He hurt Silvie. You know that I've been demonstrating self-control. You know he's been messing with me ever since we crossed paths and every time we cross paths. He crossed the line. A sin is a sin, but some sins hurt more and cost more.*

I should have been visiting my grandmother, but instead I was out seeking vengeance. Lord he brutally raped someone I love. I know I'm not you Lord, but he had to be stopped before he hurt or killed someone else. Please. I beg you. Spare my grandmother. I say out loud as tears drop from my face. An older black woman on the train comes over to me and hugs me. One human sensing the need of another human. It didn't matter that we didn't know each other. I didn't matter that she didn't know what I was crying about. She saw my need and comforted me.

I arrive at MGH and I'm given my nana's floor and room number. As I'm in the elevator, I wonder if I asked for Silvie's room out of instinct. I honestly couldn't be too sure if I asked for my grandmother or not. My mind is all over the place. Today has been a rough day.

When I enter the room, I see Silvie holding my grandmother's hand and reading the Bible to her. What are the odds of both of them being in the same room? I don't know and I don't care. I'm just grateful. My grandmother is in Silvie's room resting on the bed that was previously vacant. She looks peaceful.

"Hi Elijah," Silvie says smiling.

"Hi Silvie. How is she? Can she talk?"

"Who? Mrs. Joseph? I'm not sure if she can talk, but she was awake when she got here. The Jamaican nurse said that she had a stroke."

"Damn, her face looks distorted. It's like one side needs a face lift," I say.

"That's what often happens when you have a stroke, but that doesn't mean that she won't get back what she lost. My God is a powerful God. I came over to just pray with her. She kept staring at me when she arrived. It was as if she knew me. What's your sudden interest in older women who experienced strokes?" She says light-heartedly.

"Silvie."

"Yes, Elijah?"

"What's my name?"

"What do you mean what's your name? You just heard me call you Elijah."

"What's my full name Silvie?" I ask.

"Oh, Elijah Joseph. Why are you asking me your name?"

"I'm asking you my name and answering your question simultaneously."

"I don't get it. How is your name the answer to my question?"

"Because you are praying with my grandmother." I say smiling.

"Oh my God! This is Nana! I had no idea. I didn't even think about the fact that she had the same last name as you. Oh Elijah, I'm so sorry. I shouldn't have asked you that. That was so insensitive of me. Please accept my apology." Silvie says sincerely.

"It's ok. I'd wonder why I was asking about another woman instead of my woman. How are you feeling? Are you ok? How's your head? How's your pain below the waist line?"

"I'm healing. I took a Plan B. I couldn't risk the chance of being pregnant by my rapist."

"You don't have to explain yourself to me. You do what is right for you. I'd have your back no matter what."

"Really?" she asks softly.

"Yes really. I want to let you know that he will never do that to you again. You don't have to be fearful of him coming back. I took care of that."

"You took care of what Elijah? You're not telling me that you killed a man are you?"

"First of all, I wouldn't consider that animal a man. Second of all, NO! I wouldn't kill anyone."

"Thank God. I wouldn't want to worry about being married to you and one day that coming back to haunt you. I couldn't have my husband in jail."

"Your husband, huh? You thinking that far ahead?"

"Yup," she says with finality.

"Well ok then future Mrs. Joseph. I guess I'm going to have to wife you up before someone else tries to take my spot," I say laughing, but I'm serious.

"You better hurry up. You know there's a line of applicants waiting for you to be fired." I laugh with her.

"You know, I have some very good news. A lot has happened over the last few days." I pause.

I look over at my grandmother and see her eyes are open. She lifts her right arm motioning for me to come over. I rush over to her bed and hold her hand.

"Nana, I was so worried about you. They called me and I knew something was wrong. I prayed the entire way here Nana." Then I hug her.

She can't talk. She is making sounds, but can't formulate any words. I can see that she is frustrated. I tell her that it will take time and she's going to have to be patient. I tell her that I have some news for her. First, I introduce Silvie to her as my girlfriend. Silvie comes over with paper and pen.

"Just because you can't talk doesn't mean you can't communicate." Silvie says to Nana.

She smiles, but only one side turns up. Nana writes, "Lijah you sure work quick."

I crack up. I tell Nana and Silvie at the same time about my last few days. I left nothing out including the part about Slick.

Nana writes something else down. It takes her a while. When she's done, it reads:

"Lijah so proud of you 'bout job. Happy for you, 'bout new boo. Shitting my pants 'bout lottery and God would have forgiven you if you killed him."

Silvie reads it and laughs. "Mrs. Joseph you sure do have a sense of humor."

"She has a sassy mouth. That's what she has," I say jokingly as I notice her middle finger up at me.

An older gentleman comes through the door. I recognize him as the man that was in her room when I visited her. The one that she said didn't have to leave just because I was there. His name is Rufus. Nana is visibly happy. She waves me off. He greets us and then kisses my grandmother on her head. She shuts her eyes and a tear rolls down. He hugs my grandmother. You can clearly see the love between them. Silvie pulls me over to her side of the room and pulls the curtain between their beds to give my nana some privacy.

"I'm not going back to my apartment. Well I'm not sleeping there at least. I spoke to the manager of the apartment complex and he has another two bedroom that I can rent in Cambridge. It's more money, but I told him that I'll take it. I can't sleep in that place."

"You don't ever have to go back there. I'll make sure all your things get moved to the new apartment. You can count on me Silvie. I got your back."

"And my heart Lijah," she sings.

"Hey, hey, hey. Only my Nana gets to call me Lijah." She can see I'm kidding. Silvie can call me anything she wants as long as she calls me her man. I lean over and kiss her on her lips softly. She reciprocates with her tongue. I feel nothing but pure love for this woman. I've loved her before she knew I existed. I thought that I was invisible to her. But she was able to see me. She took a risk and gave me a chance. She didn't succumb to the stereotype of homeless men. She believes in the potential of people over people's circumstance. I am not my circumstance. Then I hear Rufus calling me over.

"Elijah, your grandmother has something for you."

I walk over to the other side of the curtain. She's sitting up now. Rufus hands me a bag. It's kind of heavy. I can't imagine what she's giving me and why it's here with her at the hospital. Rufus answers what I was questioning inside of my head.

"I knew that you'd be here at some point to see your grandmother. So, I went into her room and grabbled this bag from her closet. She was saving it for the next time you visited her at the nursing home."

"Thank you, Rufus." I say truly appreciative.

When I open it, and see what's inside, I look to see if God is sitting somewhere in the room. The bag has a hat, cap, t-shirt and hoodie that says Genetically Resilient. Not only does it have the apparel, but it also has the novels *Bitter*, *Still Bitter* and *Bitter Family Secrets*, the complete trilogy. I thought that was it, but there was another book in there. This book had the word STEREOTYPED written in bright red with what looks like a slave census in the background. I quickly skim the back cover and learn that it is a book about black men and how they live their lives rejecting and internalizing the stereotype. Each book is signed by the author Vick Breedy.

I jump up and kiss my grandmother at least ten times.

"That author lady came to the nursing home and read some of her book to us. She also was selling clothes. Your grandmother said that she knew that this would be something you'd have enjoyed. She said she remembered seeing you reading one of the books by Vick Breedy. She couldn't remember which one, so she got them all, including all the clothes. Anything for her Lijah."

I pull the t-shirt out of the bag and put it over my grandmother like a blanket. She motions for me to get it off her. Then she looks at Rufus. He comes over with another bag. It has her personal belongings. It also has her own Genetically Resilient V-neck t-shirt. She also bought Vick Breedy's book *Bitter*. I smile. I see that there's a book mark in it. She's already started reading it.

"It's a juicy read, huh Nana?"

The four of us spend the rest of the night enjoying each other's company despite the circumstance. Shit can always be worse. We still have to praise God during the rough times and then tap into our bounce back magic to get through it.

Peter:

I look at my Facebook notifications and can't believe the shit that I am reading. My sister, the crackhead, is out here spreading lies and my boy Shawn done lost his motherfucking mind. I don't appreciate Nakia reaching out to my sister to get dirt on me and Shawn. What we did when we were in junior high doesn't mean shit. We were kids. I didn't know any better. I told him that I wanted to practice on him so that I could be ready when I got a girl to give it up to me. Shawn was my best-friend so he agreed. That was it. It was only one time. That shit don't mean I'm a faggot. It's none of anyone's business anyway. Since, my sister is a crackhead, I deny the accusations. I post that she'll say or do anything for a hit. Not much has changed about her since childhood. She's always been a selfish, manipulative, lying bitch.

Once I post that, things settle down and then folks start commenting on fucked up shit that remember my sister doing back in the day. What I can't get over is that my boy flipped the fuck out. That conniving bitch deserved it though. Since she went live, everybody saw her get choked the fuck out. When she dropped the phone, it was still positioned so that you could see what was going on from the floor looking up. This Nigger is certifiably crazy. He was choking Nakia, but called her Donna. He kept saying never will you hurt me again. I do believe that he would have killed her if a neighbor hadn't called the police after she threw the pink paint on him. Yo, that shit was mad funny! I replayed it over like five times.

What I can't get over is that Oliver isn't mine. It some other dude's kid. It's the dude that they say raped her. How the fuck can you get raped by a man you already have a child by. I don't believe that she was raped. He might have hit her for mouthing off. I know she has a smart-ass mouth, but I don't think he raped her. She's lying. Why should anyone trust her? After all, she lied for six years about Oliver being mine. If she'll lie about that, she'll lie about anything.

I thought Silvie was different. I held her to higher standard. She's just as bad, if not worse than the rest of the hoes I've dealt with. I am kind of conflicted about the information. If I found out about Oliver before I spent the day with him, I might have been able to walk away with no regrets. I was kind of looking forward to being a better dad. I did tell God that I would. When I said that, I thought Oliver was mine. His biological daddy is probably going to jail. He'll never see that nigger. I feel bad for the kid. He has a lying ass mother, a hating ass uncle and a criminal for a daddy. I can't let my little homie be in that environment with no respite. Once I calm down some, I'll call Silvie and find out what she wants for Oliver. I can't make any promises, but I might be willing to take him out every other week. Black boys need their dads. When they don't have them, they need other black men to step up. I never had that. I believe that if I had, I'd be a very different man.

Shawn:

"I told her to shut up! She wouldn't stop! She just kept talking and talking. I couldn't take it. I had to make her stop talking."

The police are handcuffing me.

"You have the right to remain silent."

I talk over the police officers as they read me my Miranda.

"Wait, I can't go to jail. I have to get to work. I have some data reports that need to be in by today. I can't go to jail. I have to get to work," I say whining.

"Your black ass can kiss that job goodbye. Once they see that Facebook video that the victim posted, nobody is going to want to hire you. That's ok though. You'll be in prison with the rest of your homies. I swear you people just go from the projects to the prison and press repeat cycle."

Another officer adds his two cents.

"Don't worry you'll feel right at home. There are a whole bunch of men waiting for a new bitch to bend over. I think she said you were a bottom, right?" He says laughing like my life is a joke.

She's back. She's whispering to me.

Is that how you're going to let those white boys talk to you? The one that called you a bottom has a pen in his top pocket. You should have grabbed it and stabbed him in the neck with it. Now you're going to have to do something else. Remember, no one gets away with hurting you. No one. Not even the police. When he gets close you know what to do."

The officer that that ridiculed me for being a bottom, whispers in my ear.

"I wish you reached for your phone. That way I could have put you in the ground with the rest of those stupid niggers y'all be marching and making bunch of noise about."

"You know what to do." she whispers in my other ear.

I stand there. This time she yells.

"ATTACK!"

Elijah:

I'm on my way to Silvie's apartment. Today is moving day. I promise her that I would get her moved in and that's what I'm going to do. I met her brother Jean while I was at the hospital. He seemed like a cool dude. He had his girlfriend Imani with him. She's from Maryland. They're in a long-distance relationship but the chemistry I witnessed between the two of them has me thinking that one of them will be relocating soon enough.

I've had such a busy week. I started my new job. I've been trying to coordinate Silvie's move. I've been making sure Nana gets the services she needs. She's been transferred to a rehabilitation center. She's getting intensive speech, physical and occupational therapy. I've been dying to get to the gym. I left Shawn a message to see if he wants to work out this weekend.

As I browse the Twitter feed, I see another headline about cops shooting a black man. A police officer was killed by a laceration to his neck. The man that they had in custody bit Officer Anderson and like a dog, he wouldn't let go. *Did they just refer a black man to a dog?* The police reacted by shooting him thirty times. Both the officer and the assailant were pronounced dead at the scene. This shit sounds crazy to me. I skim the article to find out who this black man is. My heart sinks as I read the name.

Shawn Carson.

Made in the USA
Columbia, SC
12 July 2018